"I need a favor, Tucker."

"A favor." Tucker leaned back in his chair and looked at Maggie. "A big favor or a little favor?"

She bit her lip. "Pretty big. But temporary."

A big, temporary favor. He shrugged. "Sure, babe, anything for you. What's the favor?"

"I want you to marry me."

Stunned, he stared at her. Marry Maggie? He couldn't quite wrap his mind around the thought.

"You want me to marry you."

"That's right." She looked at him hopefully. "So, will you?"

Dear Reader,

I've been wanting to tell Maggie Barnes's story since she walked onto the page in *Somewhere in Texas*. But her story was always a mystery to me. When she found an infant, abandoned beside her patrol car, I suddenly knew what Maggie's heart's desire was—a family of her own.

There are a lot of obstacles for Maggie, and convincing her old friend Tucker Jones to marry her so she can foster parent the baby is only the first of them. A happy bachelor, Tucker isn't at all anxious to be married, but if it will help Maggie get what she wants, he's willing to go along with her.

Neither of them realizes how hard it will be to maintain a platonic relationship—especially when they start falling for each other. But both of them know that giving in to their passion risks their friendship....

I hope you enjoy Maggie and Tucker's journey. I love to hear from readers. Write me at P.O. Box 131704, Tyler, TX 75713-1704 or e-mail eve@evegaddy.net and visit my Web site at www.evegaddy.net.

Eve Gaddy

BABY BE MINE
Eve Gaddy

HARLEQUIN®

TORONTO • NEW YORK • LONDON
AMSTERDAM • PARIS • SYDNEY • HAMBURG
STOCKHOLM • ATHENS • TOKYO • MILAN • MADRID
PRAGUE • WARSAW • BUDAPEST • AUCKLAND

ISBN-13: 978-0-373-78229-1
ISBN-10:　　0-373-78229-2

BABY BE MINE

This edition published by arrangement with Harlequin Books S.A.

® and TM are trademarks of the publisher. Trademarks indicated with
® are registered in the United States Patent and Trademark Office, the
Canadian Trade Marks Office and in other countries.

www.eHarlequin.com

Printed in U.S.A.

ABOUT THE AUTHOR

Eve Gaddy is an award-winning author of more than fifteen novels. She lives in east Texas with her husband and her incredibly spoiled golden retriever, Maverick, who is convinced he's her third child. She is currently hard at work writing more Superromance books.

Books by Eve Gaddy

HARLEQUIN SUPERROMANCE

903–COWBOY COME HOME
962–FULLY ENGAGED
990–A MAN OF HIS WORD
1031–TROUBLE IN TEXAS
1090–A MARRIAGE MADE IN TEXAS
1122–CASEY'S GAMBLE
1276–SOMEWHERE IN TEXAS
1313–THAT NIGHT IN TEXAS
1367–REMEMBER TEXAS
1457–THE CHRISTMAS BABY

Don't miss any of our special offers. Write to us at the following address for information on our newest releases.

Harlequin Reader Service
U.S.: 3010 Walden Ave., P.O. Box 1325, Buffalo, NY 14269
Canadian: P.O. Box 609, Fort Erie, Ont. L2A 5X3

This book is for Mary Ellen Brown, my best friend
through so much and for so many years.
I'm blessed to have you in my life.

Acknowledgments

Many thanks to Dr. Nancy Lieb for once again
being my source for all things obstetric and
gynecological. And many thanks to
Meridith Hayes for answering my legal questions.
As well as many thanks to Justine Davis for
answering my questions about cops, women in
particular. Any mistakes about any of these things
are mine alone. I also want to thank
Kathy Carmichael and Kathy Garbera
for critiquing and listening, and especially
for helping me when I get stuck. Y'all rock!

CHAPTER ONE

THE LOVINGLY RESTORED, guardsman-blue '64 Ford Mustang convertible blew into town doing fifty-two in a forty. Twenty seconds later Maggie Barnes nailed him. Lights flashing, siren wailing, the sweet, high sound cops loved and everyone else feared, she drove up behind him and pointed to the curb when he looked in the rearview mirror. She read his lips and laughed out loud.

Sometimes she really loved being a cop. When the speeder was Tucker Jones it only made life that much sweeter. Her old friend Tucker could always make her laugh. And since today was Friday and Valentine's Day, Maggie could use some entertainment.

Valentine's Day was highly overrated, in her opinion. The fact she was single and not dating anyone had nothing to do with it, she assured herself. She didn't like it because it was a stupid holiday designed to make money for florists, jewelers and producers of chocolate. Besides that, work usually sucked on Valentine's Day. You could never tell what crazy thing someone would get into their head to do and then she would have to clean up the mess.

Seeing Tucker Jones's beautiful blue eyes and listening to his latest excuse about why he was speeding seemed like a much better alternative to wondering what new disaster was waiting for her later that evening.

Since it was a near-record warm day for February, he'd been driving with the top down and was waiting for her when she reached the car, his fingers beating a tattoo on the car door. The car, like its owner, was bad, gorgeous and sexy. She knew all about that badass car of Tucker's, because he'd told her in exhaustive detail on more than one occasion how he'd rebuilt and restored it.

"Hey, Maggie."

"Hey, Tucker."

"Is there a problem?" he asked. Of course, he knew perfectly well why she'd stopped him.

She took off her sunglasses and hooked them on her shirt pocket. "Well, now, there sure is."

"I wasn't speeding. Your radar must be broken."

"I didn't say I pulled you over for speeding."

"Why did you, then?"

"Because you were speeding. Again." Maggie looked him over and smiled. "Fifty-two in a forty. You're busted, Tucker. License and registration, please." She reflected that she ought to have that information memorized by now.

"I know a good lawyer. I'll get out of it. Save yourself the trouble." He handed her his driver's license and reached in the glove compartment for the vehicle registration.

Maggie laughed. Tucker was a lawyer and he undoubtedly would get out of the ticket. That fact never stopped him from arguing, though. Or her from giving him a ticket if she wanted. "You know what they say about a lawyer who defends himself."

"Having a fool for a client? Witty. Very witty. Have I mentioned I really go for a woman in uniform?" He gave her a wicked, sexy grin.

Damn, he was cute. And he knew it, too. She started writing information on the ticket. "Only every time I've ever pulled you over. Too many to count."

"Have I ever said I really go for beautiful redheads in uniform? Especially a cop uniform?"

She nodded. "Also every time I've pulled you

over." She glanced at him and added, "Funny thing, that's the only time you ever mention it."

"It was worth a try." He gave her his most charming smile, which she admitted was something to see.

"Did you have a reason for speeding?" He almost certainly didn't. Unless it was because he liked his cars as fast as he liked his women.

"Why do I need a reason? No one can drive this car and not speed. It's unnatural."

Maggie snorted.

"Doesn't the fact that we've been friends since high school make a difference?"

"Tucker, if I only stopped people I didn't know, I'd never stop anyone. Then the chief would fire me and what would I do? Sell shoes?"

"Come on, Mags, have a heart."

"Don't call me 'Mags,'" she said. He knew she hated it and did it to annoy her. "Cops give tickets. Cops don't have hearts."

"I know one cop who does. You." He looked at her soulfully and, she hated to admit, it was proving effective.

She handed him the warning ticket. "You could be right. But don't let it get out."

He grabbed her hand and kissed it lavishly. "You're one in a million. Run away with me and be my love. We'll go to Mexico." He kissed her hand again. "Or Aruba. Or Tahiti. We'll go—"

Laughing, she pulled her hand away. "Stop that, you fool. I'm on duty here."

"You won't run off with me?" He looked incredibly disappointed.

Maggie shook her head. "Sorry. You'd be flirting with another woman before the plane touched down. Possibly before it left."

"Oh, come on, Maggie. I'm not that bad."

"Ha."

"I'm not. You sound like my mother."

"Gee, thanks." Maggie didn't much care for Tucker's mother, and the feeling was more than mutual. Eileen Jones always looked at Maggie as if she were something nasty stuck to the bottom of her shoe. "What's she done this time?"

"Same thing she always does. 'Darling, you must stop this incessant womanizing and settle down. I know just the girl,'" he said in a fair imitation of his mother's accent.

"How many women has she introduced you to over the years?" Maggie asked. "Hundreds?"

"I've lost count. I've been going out with the latest in a long list. Several times."

Maggie raised an eyebrow. "Sounds serious."

"Well, it's not." He scowled. "Damn it, that doesn't mean I'm a womanizer."

"Seems a little harsh," Maggie agreed. "I'd call you a player, myself, but incessant player-izing doesn't have quite the same ring."

"Very funny. The woman has an obsession with having grandchildren. You'd think she had one foot in the grave."

"You can't blame your mother for wanting grandkids. You are her only child and you'd have pretty babies."

He put his hand over his heart and patted. "Be still. Maggie Barnes just paid me a compliment."

"Don't let it go to your head," she advised him. "It's fat enough already."

"I think the term is *swelled.*"

"Fat, swelled, makes no difference to me." Surprisingly, Tucker wasn't conceited, she just liked to tease him. Oh, he knew he was good-looking and that women liked him. They'd been after him since high school so he could hardly help knowing it. But Tucker believed most women pursued him because he'd grown up with money and then made a bundle on his own, when he'd practiced in San Antonio before moving back to the Aransas City area. She suspected there was a story there, but beyond an odd comment or two, he'd never told her.

Her radio squawked and she pressed the button down in response. "Crap," Maggie said when she heard the code. "I've got to go. Cheer up, Tucker. At least you don't have to go break up a domestic disturbance."

"Maggie." He put his hand on her arm. "Be careful, okay?"

"Always am," she told him. "But thanks for worrying."

TUCKER WONDERED NOW and then what would have happened if he and Maggie had ever hooked up. They wouldn't still be friends, that was a given. He'd remained friendly with women he'd dated, but never what he'd call truly friends. Since he valued his friendship with Maggie as much as she did, she was probably smart to make sure it stayed that way.

He watched her walk back to her car, admiring the way she moved. Most of the time, he just saw his old friend Maggie when he looked at her, but every once in a while he remembered she was a woman, and a damned attractive one to boot.

He started the car and pulled onto the road,

heading for his parents' place in Key Allegro to drop off some legal papers. He thought about Maggie again and the call that had come in for her. He knew she could take care of herself. She was a good, experienced cop. But shit happened. A year or so ago she'd had to shoot and kill a man who had already shot a friend of hers and who was also trying to kill his estranged wife. Domestic-violence calls could get out of hand quickly and he didn't want another one to go sour on Maggie.

She'd handled it in the past, though. He had to trust she'd handle whatever happened in the future.

Maggie wasn't a girly-girl, but she was definitely feminine. She was a Tae Kwon Do black belt, and although he was as well, she'd kicked his ass on more than one occasion. He'd also heard rumors that she'd taken up boxing lately, though he hadn't verified that.

Twenty minutes later he pulled up to his parents' waterfront home, parked and went up the walk.

"Darling, you're late," his mother said as she opened the door and enveloped him in a scented embrace.

"Late? You didn't know I was coming."

"But of course I did. You told your father and he told me." She put her arm through his and led him into the living room. "And someone else you know is here with me," she added meaningfully.

A woman stood with her back to them, a spill of long, red hair waving to her shoulders. *Maggie? Impossible…. He'd just left her, and she hadn't been headed this way.*

"Isabella?" He realized who she was as she turned around. "I wasn't expecting to see you here."

Isabella was the woman he'd mentioned to Maggie. They'd gone out a number of times since his mother had introduced them. She was beautiful, cultured, sweet and intelligent. There wasn't a reason in the world he shouldn't have taken her to bed, but he just hadn't been ready to take the relationship to that level. If they became lovers, Isabella would read more into it than he was ready for.

She smiled. "I came by to see Eileen on opera-committee business. When she mentioned you were coming by I thought I'd stay and say hello."

He took the hand she held out and, because she expected it, kissed her cheek. Turning to his mother he said, "I just stopped by to leave you these papers. Don't forget to tell Dad," he said, walking over to lay the packet down on the grand piano.

He stayed and talked a while, then, since his mother and Isabella both expected it, made a date for the following night. Isabella left shortly thereafter, and he congratulated himself on successfully getting his mother off his back once more.

"Tucker, stay a moment," Eileen said when he would have left. "Isabella is a lovely girl, isn't she?"

"Sure, she's pretty," Tucker said warily.

"Her family is from Fort Worth, originally. Her parents are on the boards of a number of museums."

Tucker tilted his head. "Mom, why would you think I give a flip about what Isabella's family does?"

She made the *tsk* sound that generally annoyed the hell out of him. "You seem very interested in her. I thought you'd like to know something about her background, in case she hasn't told you, that is. I believe her family is quite wealthy, which I'm certain she won't have mentioned."

He bit down on the urge to say, *No, that would*

be vulgar, wouldn't it? "I'm not sure why you're telling me all this. I've dated her a few times. Nothing serious."

"But it could be. Oh, Tucker, she's exactly the type of woman I can see you with."

Tucker pinched the bridge of his nose, wondering how he could get out of the house without telling his mother to butt out. Because if he did that she'd get her feelings hurt, and while she wouldn't cry, she'd make him feel like the biggest jerk on the planet.

Before he could think of a good response, Eileen said, "I simply want you to think about the fact that Isabella would be a perfect match for you. And that you're certainly old enough to consider settling down."

He wasn't in love with Isabella, though. But then, he didn't really believe he'd fall in love again. He'd been burned badly enough to make him a little cynical about love. He wasn't going into that subject with his mother, however. She'd find a way to demolish his arguments. She always did, at least on this subject.

"I'll think about it," he said. Which, of course, he wouldn't. He had no desire to get married, but he knew better than to argue with the brick wall of his mother's will. Much easier to avoid her for a while.

He got away without too much more trouble. But instead of thinking of Isabella, he found himself thinking of an entirely different woman all the way home. A certain redheaded cop he'd known since high school.

Maybe he could talk Maggie into being friends with benefits. He thought about that a moment. Then shook his head regretfully. No, their friendship was more important to him than any momentary pleasure. Besides, she'd laugh herself sick if he proposed it. And then she'd invite him to spar with her and kick his ass for good measure.

CHAPTER TWO

"I CAN HELP YOU and your kids get into a women's shelter," Maggie said. "Just say the word and I can arrange it. You and the children could be there and safe before your husband returns."

"I don't need a shelter," Sara Myers said. "Jasper would never hurt me or the kids."

What do you call that shiner he gave you? Maggie wondered. *A love tap?* That must have hurt like hell. Maggie didn't hold out much hope that the woman would leave her abusive husband. She'd had too much experience with this sort of thing and she could see the woman wasn't ready to admit the guy would likely only get worse over time.

"I told you I fell," Sara insisted. "Jasper didn't lay a hand on me. I'm sorry for your trouble."

Maggie sighed, acknowledging defeat. The neighbors had called this one in, reporting a disturbance in the apartment next door. By the time Maggie arrived, the woman's abusive spouse was long gone. Probably drunk and gone off to get even drunker, Maggie thought, and then he'd come home and whale on the poor woman some more.

"Call us if you need us. And here's my cell number in case you change your mind about that shelter." She handed the woman her card.

Sara showed her to the door. "He's a good man, he really is. He's upset about losing his job. That's all."

Maggie didn't reply. What could she say that she hadn't already told the woman during the half hour she'd spent with her? Certain that the beating had been "just this once," the lady wasn't listening. Maggie hated domestic-abuse cases. Hated that she couldn't do more to help the victims. But Sara had refused to admit the truth, and with the abuser not even being present, Maggie's hands were tied.

Happy Valentine's Day, she thought grimly, walking to her cruiser in the deepening twilight. An annoying day, topped off by an abused woman who wouldn't accept her help. She'd been a cop too long to jinx herself by saying the day couldn't get worse, because in police work, it could and frequently did.

As she neared her cruiser she heard a baby crying. She looked around but didn't see another soul in the parking lot. The noise sounded as if it was coming from near her patrol car. As she reached it, Maggie stopped short, nearly tripping over the car seat that sat beside the driver's door.

"Well, what do we have here?" she said as she squatted down to see the baby in the car seat. "What's wrong, sweetheart? Where's your mother?"

The infant was a girl, judging from the pink blanket she was wrapped in. She couldn't be more than two months old, if that. She touched the baby's cheek. It didn't feel too cool so maybe she hadn't been here long. She looked around again but whoever had left the child was either long gone or hiding.

She scanned some bushes a short distance away, but couldn't see much in the gloom. She started to walk over to look more closely, but the baby was cranked up and crying in earnest now and clearly needed her attention. She squatted down again, spotted a pacifier and put it in the little girl's mouth. That quieted her, at least for the moment.

There was a note pinned to the blanket.

Maggie shined her flashlight on it to read the printed block letters.

Please take care of my baby.
He said he'd kill her if I
keep her. Her name is Grace.

Holy moly. Maggie stared at the baby, who was fretting and looked like she was winding up to cry again. Probably hungry, poor little thing. Then she noticed there were a couple of bottles in the car seat as well as some diapers.

Maggie stood, torn between wanting to check out possible witnesses and the fact that she couldn't leave the child. She sure as hell didn't intend to cart the baby with her while she talked to people.

She popped her trunk open and pulled out a pair of thin latex gloves and put them on. Then she took the note off and bagged it, to take it to the police lab. She would probably have the car seat and bottles dusted for fingerprints, and she didn't want to contaminate the surfaces with her own.

She picked up the car seat and put the baby in the cruiser since it had gotten a little chilly. Then she keyed in the mike and said, "Requesting backup at the Wayside Apartments, two-seventy-five Fifth Street. I have an abandoned infant."

"What's that you say?" Allison, the dispatcher, said. "A baby?"

"That's right. I found her sitting in her car seat right beside my door. I need some help to check out the building for witnesses." Just then the baby—Grace, the note had said—spit out her pacifier and began to wail. "Send me the backup as quick as you can. I have to go."

Turning on the interior light, she took the baby out of the car seat and settled her in the crook of her arm. When she gave her the bottle, Grace sucked on it greedily. Maggie wondered if the mother was still hanging around, trying to see what was going to happen. Or had she simply set the carrier down and walked off, trusting the cops would come back to the car before long? Either way, Maggie didn't like it. Abandonment was a crime, plain and simple.

Grace was a beautiful baby. Fine blond hair, dark blue eyes like all babies had at first, perfect rosebud mouth. She looked well cared for, Maggie admitted. And she was so sweet. But then, all babies were sweet. Her nieces and nephews certainly were.

She stifled a pang, remembering she

wouldn't be seeing either her sister Lorna or her kids—Bobby, Jeannette and baby Summer—as often as she had in the past. Her sister's husband had recently been transferred and the whole family had moved away. To Florida, of all places. If Maggie saw them at holidays from now on, she'd be lucky.

Now Maggie's parents were thinking about following them. Her dad was a fisherman but he'd been talking about retiring and doing something else. Maggie couldn't imagine it, but her mother sounded set on moving.

Maggie loved her mother but sometimes she really resented knowing that her mother didn't think she'd ever get married and have children of her own. "You're just not domestic, Maggie." A refrain she'd heard from her mother and sister for years. Her dad never said it, but then, he didn't talk a lot anyway.

Although Maggie admitted she wasn't a regular domestic goddess by any means, she didn't see why that precluded her having a family of her own. Of course, she had to find a man in order to do that, and that didn't seem likely anytime soon.

After Grace finished the bottle, Maggie burped her. She thought about putting her back in her seat, but there was still no sign of backup, so she simply held her until Grace fell asleep. "Don't you worry, honey," she murmured to the sleeping baby. "Maggie will make sure you're taken care of while we look for your mama."

AN HOUR LATER Maggie held a crying baby Grace in one arm, while holding a phone receiver against her ear. "No, we haven't located the mother," she told her friend Nina Baker, a social worker at Child Protective Services. "We've barely had time to question anyone. There were no witnesses. Or at least, no one who'll admit to seeing anything."

"Have you identified the baby yet?"

"No. I'm about to take her footprint and see if we can find a match at any of the area hospitals. But even if we identify the baby that doesn't mean I can find the mother. I couldn't get any useable prints from the note or the car seat or the bottles she left."

"Sounds like it might take a while to find the mother, then."

"You got that right. This baby needs someplace to stay as soon as possible. She's exhausted and needs somewhere to sleep besides in her car seat at the police station."

"I'll get right on it, Maggie," Nina said. "I'll call you back as soon as I've located foster care for her."

"Do you think that will be a problem?"

"Oh, no, I'm sure it won't be. I'll call you back as soon as I find a home."

Thirty minutes later, Nina still hadn't gotten back to her so Maggie called her. "Nina, what's going on? This baby needs to get out of here."

"I'm sorry, but I'm having a little problem finding someone to keep her on such short notice. The foster parents we usually turn to in this situation are ill and I'm having to call all around the area."

"You haven't found anyone?"

"Well, not yet," Nina admitted. "But I've contacted another—"

"Look, let me take her home with me," Maggie interrupted. "This is stupid. She needs a bath, she needs some food and she needs to get the hell out of here so she can sleep. I'm telling you, the poor little baby is exhausted."

"Well… Are you sure? I could take her myself, but—"

"Just let me take care of her, Nina."

"I suppose that would be all right," she said, still hesitant. "But aren't you on duty?"

"I cleared it with the chief to go off shift early. I'll take her home with me and you can let me know when you've found a foster family for her."

"Thanks, Maggie. You're a lifesaver."

"Come on, sweetheart," she said to the sobbing baby. "You're going home with Maggie. We're going to get you all fixed up."

JUST BEFORE SHE LEFT the station Maggie called Delilah Randolph. Delilah and her husband, Cameron, owned the waterfront restaurant and bar The Scarlet Parrot.

"Delilah, it's Maggie," she said when her friend answered. "I need a favor."

"Sure, Maggie. What is it?"

"I need to borrow some diapers and formula and bottles until I have a chance to buy some. And maybe a playpen or something else for the baby to sleep in."

"What baby?"

"I found an abandoned baby a few hours ago and CPS couldn't find anyone to keep her tonight. I'm taking her home with me and thought maybe you could help me out."

"Someone abandoned their infant? How terrible."

"It happens," Maggie said. "Although it's

more often newborns who are abandoned. This little girl is a couple of months old, I think."

"I'll bring some things and meet you at your house. I've got some clothes, too. A footed sleeper and something for her to wear tomorrow. Any idea what size she is?"

Maggie checked the outfit Grace wore and told Delilah the size.

"Got it. I'll see what I have and borrow whatever else we need from my sister-in-law."

"Great—thanks, Delilah. See you in a few."

An hour later Maggie put a bathed, fed and freshly clothed baby Grace to bed in the borrowed playpen turned crib. Delilah had stayed to help her and was waiting for Maggie in the kitchen.

"I put her on her back," Maggie said, walking into the room. "That's what they tell you, isn't it?"

"That's right. Until she can turn over she should sleep on her back."

"Want some hot chocolate?"

"If you're having some."

As Maggie took out the mugs and ingredients, Delilah asked, "What's going to happen to Grace now?"

"She'll go into foster care until we locate the mother. If we don't find the mother…" Maggie poured milk and chocolate into the mugs and stirred them. "I suppose she'll eventually wind up being adopted. Who knows how long that will be, though?" She stuck the mugs in the microwave and turned it on.

"It's odd, but the baby didn't look neglected. Or abused. I looked for bruises or other signs when we bathed her. I'd say she'd been well taken care of."

"That's what I thought, too. No signs of abuse at all."

"Why would her mother abandon her? I can't imagine abandoning Johnny."

"She left a note saying 'he' threatened to kill the baby and asked that she be taken care of. Thought the police should be able to do that, I imagine. That's why she left her by the patrol car."

"I'd have left him, then. Not the baby."

"Not everyone's as brave as you were, Delilah. Or as smart to get out while you could. But yeah, that's what I'd have done, too."

Delilah laughed. "I wasn't brave, I was scared for my life. That's why I ran."

Delilah had fled an abusive marriage. A man who had already murdered his first wife. She was on the run when she'd met Cameron and eventually married him after her husband was killed. By Maggie.

The microwave dinged so she took out the mugs and set one in front of her friend.

"It still bothers you, doesn't it?" Delilah said. "That you had to shoot him. And that he died."

"No." She shook her head. "I've made peace with it. He gave me no choice but to shoot him. I just wish there had been another way to settle things, that's all."

Delilah reached for her hand and squeezed it. "You saved all of us that day, Maggie. Me, Cam and Gabe. I said it then and I'll say it now. Thank you."

"Why are we talking about that?" Maggie said gruffly. "I did my job and there's no gratitude necessary." She took a sip of hot chocolate. "Now let me ask you something."

Delilah sat back, smiling. "Okay. What?"

"Do you think it would be totally crazy if I applied to be Grace's foster mother?"

CHAPTER THREE

THE NEXT DAY, Nina still hadn't found foster care for Grace, so Maggie kept her that day and night. It didn't take long to realize that keeping the little girl had turned her heart to mush.

She'd always loved children. Once, she'd imagined that someday she'd find a man, marry him and have a family with him. But she was thirty-four and beginning to think that scenario was never going to happen. Even so, with one notable exception, she'd never considered single parenthood. Until now.

The crazy idea she'd shared with Delilah had really taken hold in her mind. Delilah hadn't thought it sounded too wild, and had urged her to go for it if that was really what she wanted. But although Delilah herself had been in the foster care system briefly, she knew no more than Maggie did about becoming a foster parent.

Why shouldn't she apply to care for Grace?

She had a good job and was perfectly capable of caring for a child. She'd have to work something out about her hours and child care while she was at work, but there were working single mothers everywhere. Her idea was only bolstered by the thought of the precious little girl adrift in the system.

Maggie believed there was a very good chance the police would track down the parents, but who knew what would happen once they did? Even if they found Grace's parents, she could very well still remain in the foster care system, depending on what the judge decided about the charges of abandonment that were sure to be brought against the mother and possibly the father, as well.

She'd talked to the chief and he'd agreed to give Maggie a few days off to take care of the baby until a more permanent solution could be reached. And in the meantime, Maggie was falling hard for baby Grace.

The morning after that, Nina called. "I found a foster home for Grace. When would be a good time for me to come pick her up?"

Never, Maggie thought, looking at the baby in her arms. Grace was smiling and blowing bubbles. "I can keep her longer. It's not a problem."

"Oh, that's sweet of you, Maggie, but I need to get her into a licensed home. Technically, I shouldn't have let you keep her, but I was in a bind, and besides, I know you."

"Nina—" She started to say something but decided what she wanted to talk about would be better discussed face-to-face. "Never mind, I'll see you in a little while."

"Any news about locating the mother?" Nina asked after she arrived at Maggie's house.

Maggie sat in her easy chair to feed Grace while she talked to Nina. She refused to think about the fact that it might be the last bottle she gave the baby.

"We know her name. The footprint matched a child born to a Carol Davis, nine and a half weeks ago. Father unknown. She named the baby Grace, which is what the note said. No luck on her last listed place of residence. She was long gone and no one remembered much about her. Or said they didn't. It was marginal housing, a hole-in-the-wall apartment complex in Corpus Christi in a bad part of town.

"According to the officer who checked all this out, Carol Davis lived there with a man, but no one knew his name or admitted to knowing anything about him. The officer got the impression he might have been a gangbanger and they were afraid to talk."

"Which would help explain why she abandoned the baby. If she's involved with a gang member who doesn't want the child it must have seemed safer to give the baby up."

"But why didn't she go through other channels? Legal channels? Why just abandon her? I'm telling you, Nina, the child has been well cared for. I don't think she was neglected in any way. So why would the woman suddenly be willing to simply walk away from her child, abandoning her in a parking lot, for God's sake?"

"I don't know. There can be a number of reasons why she might abandon the child. But until you find her we won't know. You have no idea where she went after she left the apartment complex?"

Maggie shook her head. "My department is pursuing leads, as is the Corpus Christi police department, but it's not looking good. The mother seems to have vanished. If she's living with a banger we may never find her." She burped Grace and leaned back to hold her in her arms. A rocker, that's what she needed.

"But she delivered the baby at a hospital.

Seems like you could get some information through them."

"Yes, but we didn't. Carol Davis came in as an indigent through the E.R. There's no way she had the money to cover hospital costs, and she sure as heck didn't have insurance."

"No, I suppose not. Well, good luck. It sounds like you'll need it." Nina glanced at her watch. "I need to be going. I told the Petersons I'd bring the baby over as soon as possible."

"Yeah, Nina, about that. Could I talk to you a minute?"

"Of course."

Maggie hesitated, wondering how to broach the subject. "If I were licensed for foster care, is it possible I could take care of Grace?"

Nina stared at her a moment. "You've never mentioned wanting to be a foster parent before."

"It's something I've been thinking about for a while now," Maggie said. Which wasn't a lie if a couple of days could be considered a while. "Taking care of Grace made me realize I really did want to become licensed." But she had to admit, she didn't want to be just anyone's foster mother, she wanted to be Grace's foster mother.

"Even if you do, there's no guarantee you'll be allowed to foster Grace."

She must be pretty transparent. "But there's a chance."

"Yes, of course there's a chance. Maggie, are you really serious about this?"

She nodded. "Foster parents get first shot at adopting the child, right? Assuming she comes up for adoption?"

"Yes, but—" Nina looked troubled. "First of all, you don't know that Grace will ever come up for adoption. And it's not that simple. There's a long process involved in becoming licensed as a foster parent. Training and assessment of your ability to care for children, background checks, that sort of thing. And then there's an even more intensive process to be approved as an adoptive parent. Intensive and invasive. The people who assess you pry into every part of your life. Your present, your past, your relationships with friends and family. Everything."

"I don't have any skeletons." Not just a lie, but a whopper. But her secrets were buried deep. "I'm a cop. I have a good, steady job. I'm a respectable, responsible person. Doesn't that count?"

"Well, of course, but—"

"I want to start the process now," Maggie interrupted. "Help me do this, Nina."

Nina seemed distressed. She hemmed and hawed and finally said, "You're single."

"What does that have to do with anything? I looked it up online. It says single people can be foster and adoptive parents."

"That's true." Nina bit her lip and sighed. "I wouldn't tell just anyone this, but since it's you… If there's a choice between giving a child to a single parent and giving her to a couple, the couple wins almost every time. The party line is that your marital status doesn't matter, but take it from me, it does."

"You're saying I have to be married to be Grace's foster mother. To be a foster mother, period."

"No, not at all. I see no reason why you won't be approved as a single foster parent. But I am saying your chances of getting to keep Grace are better if you're married." She hesitated. "The thing is, Grace is the type of child who everyone wants to foster or adopt. She's an infant and she's healthy. Now, if she had some sort of mental or physical problem, then that might be a different case. I'm telling you the truth, Maggie, even though it shouldn't be that way." She stood and added, "The Petersons are a great couple. Grace will be in good hands."

But she wouldn't be in Maggie's hands. It wasn't fair, damn it. It wasn't as if she could go out and stop the next man she saw and ask him to marry her. She wasn't even dating anyone, much less talking marriage. The only single men she knew very well were committed bachelors.

Single man. Committed bachelor. An idea hit her, stunning in its simplicity.

"You're not seeing anyone seriously, are you, Maggie?"

"Actually, I am. In fact, I think he's going to propose any day now." *Liar, liar,* her mind chanted. *Minor detail,* she decided. *I can fix this.*

Nina looked like she wasn't sure she believed her. "Isn't this kind of sudden? I don't remember you talking about seeing anyone special."

"But you haven't seen me in a couple of months," Maggie reminded her. "He's an old friend of mine. We started dating fairly recently, but we've known each other forever."

"Does he have a name?" Nina asked drily.

"Tucker Jones," Maggie said, stepping into deep, deep trouble.

SINCE SHE WAS still off for the day, Maggie decided to put her plan into action immediately. Anything was better than sitting around looking at all the baby stuff…and no baby to go with it. She'd watched Nina take Grace away with her heart heavy and tears threatening. At least she would be able to see the baby, though. Nina had said she'd fix it with Grace's foster parents for Maggie to visit and she'd let them know Maggie wanted to care for Grace as soon as she was approved.

As a rule, Maggie didn't cry. Since she'd become a cop there were only a handful of times she could remember crying. A couple of times when she'd worked in Dallas and a particularly brutal case had come along. She hadn't cried on the job but she sure had once she'd gone home.

Another time had been when she discovered the man she'd believed wanted to marry her had lied to her. Not only was he not divorcing his wife, but his wife was pregnant with his child. And to put the whipped cream on that dessert, the wife had gotten pregnant while Maggie was dating him.

She'd cried over him, and over her naiveté in believing his lies when he'd been stringing Maggie along. After that, she vowed never to get involved with a man who wasn't completely free. She'd kept that vow until she'd met and fallen for the love of her life. What a disaster that had been.

But Tucker Jones was as free as a bird. Well, he did say he was dating someone, but he also said he wasn't serious. Surely he hadn't managed to fall madly in love with the woman in the space of a few days. Not Tucker. He enjoyed his freedom too much.

Which could be a problem, she admitted. But it wouldn't be a real marriage, after all. He could resume all his normal activities as soon as they divorced. After she had custody of Grace.

First she had to see him, though. Since it was Sunday and she knew he rarely went to church, she called him at home. Maggie waited as the phone rang, tapping her pen on the table.

"Hey, Maggie. What's up?"

"Oh, not much," she said, keeping it casual. "How about meeting me for lunch today?"

"Today?"

Her heart sank. She really wanted to put her plan in action. "Yes. Why, do you have plans?"

"I could rearrange them if it's important."

"If you wouldn't mind, I'd really like to see you today."

"All right. When and where?"

"The Scarlet Parrot, about twelve-thirty."

"See you there."

TUCKER HAD HAD TO cancel a lunch date with Isabella but he'd done it willingly. There had been something in Maggie's voice that he couldn't quite describe. She'd sounded a little bit anxious, he thought. Something was going on with her.

He was waiting for her at the table when she walked in. Damn, she knew how to make an entrance. She wasn't in uniform and she looked nothing like a cop. Nothing like one of the guys, either. Today she wore her long, wavy red hair down around her shoulders, a lightweight white sweater that molded to her generous curves and a short, tight black skirt that made her world-class legs hard to miss, even for a man who didn't normally think about said legs.

Now he knew something was going on. Maggie didn't often dress up, at least that he'd seen, but when she did… Wow. He stood as she reached the table.

"Hi, Tucker. Thanks for meeting me," she said as she sat in the chair he'd pulled out for her.

He sat down, too. "Wouldn't miss it. You look great, Maggie."

"Thanks," she said, looking pleased.

He considered her a moment. "What are you up to?"

She smiled and flashed him a look brimming

with mischief. "Now why would you think I'm up to something? Just because I asked you to lunch?"

He'd noticed before that Maggie's hazel eyes often changed color with her mood. Tucker wasn't sure what kind of mood went with that brilliant emerald-green, but he found it more than a little fascinating.

"That's one reason," he said. And because she'd gone to some trouble to look like one of his ultimate fantasies. The thought made him feel…weird. This was Maggie, after all. "Is this like a date?" he asked suspiciously.

"Not exactly," she said, with a laugh in her voice.

"Last I checked you swore you'd never date me. You said you'd been cured of that in high school." Even all this time later, he still felt like a jerk whenever he thought about what had happened the one and only time she'd agreed to go out with him, when he'd asked her to homecoming her junior year. Even so, it was a long time to hold a grudge, in his opinion.

"I'm sure I didn't say never." She busied herself spreading her napkin out and putting it in her lap. "Besides, I told you, this isn't exactly a date."

The waitress came and took their drink order,

returning shortly with two iced teas. When she asked if they were ready to order, Maggie told her they'd like to wait.

Mystified and curious as hell, Tucker waited for Maggie to get to the point…which she didn't do.

She stirred sweetener into her tea and took a sip. "How was your date with the latest audition?"

"The latest what?" he said blankly.

"You know, the woman your mother set you up with. The one you said you'd been dating. The latest auditioner for the part of Mrs. Tucker Jones. The future mother of your children."

"Oh, Isabella. She's…nice." He took a sip of his drink, wondering where she was heading. If she was heading anywhere, which he was beginning to doubt.

"Just nice? Are you seeing her again?"

"I'm not sure. Why?" he asked. Maggie didn't normally quiz him about his dating habits. A suspicion entered his mind. "Are you trying to set me up with someone, Maggie?"

She laughed. "I guess you could say that. I just wanted to make sure you're not involved with anyone."

"You ought to know I'm not. You saw me three days ago and I wasn't then." He took another drink and continued, "If you want me to go out with a friend of yours, why didn't you just ask me over the phone? Why the lunch and all the mystery?"

"It's not that simple."

It never was. He wondered what was wrong with the woman, because there almost had to be something seriously weird about her. "Who is this woman?"

"Well, Tucker—" She met his gaze and held it with dancing green eyes. "It's me. But I don't exactly want to date you."

"Color me confused as hell. What are you talking about, Maggie?"

"I need a favor, Tucker."

A favor? Why didn't she just ask? Why all the lead-up? But knowing Maggie, she must have a reason for how she approached him. "A favor." He leaned back in his chair and looked at her. She seemed a little anxious now. "A big favor or a little favor?"

She bit her lip. "Pretty big," she admitted. "But temporary."

A big, temporary favor. He shrugged. "Sure, babe, anything for you. What's the favor?"

"I want you to marry me."

Stunned, he stared at her. Marry Maggie? He couldn't quite wrap his mind around the thought.

"You want me to marry you."

"That's right." She nodded happily, as if pleased by his perception. "So, will you?"

"Maggie…?" She looked at him hopefully. "What are you smokin'?"

CHAPTER FOUR

MAGGIE SCOWLED AT HIM. "Very funny. I'm not on drugs and you know it."

"You want me to marry you and we've never even been on a date. How crazy is that?"

"It's not crazy," she insisted, though she realized it did sound a bit…well, strange.

"Why?" When she didn't answer, he said, "Are you pregnant? Did the son of a bitch run out on you?"

"Don't be silly. Of course I'm not pregnant. It's nothing like that."

He put his face in his hands and laughed. And continued to laugh. When he finally stopped laughing he wiped his eyes and looked at her. "Okay, you really had me going for a minute. What's the joke?"

"It's not a joke. I'm dead serious."

Delilah stopped at the table. "Hi, Tucker. Hey, Maggie. Has Rachel taken your order?"

"I told her we'd wait but would you mind sending her back over?"

"I'll do better than that. What do you need?"

They both ordered the shrimp plate, a dish the Scarlet Parrot was famous for.

"How's the baby?" Delilah asked as she picked up their menus.

"She's good. They found her a foster home. Took her this morning."

"What did you decide to do?"

"I'm working on it," Maggie said, and couldn't resist glancing at Tucker. He looked thoughtful, not confused. Damn it, the man always had been quick.

Delilah smiled but didn't say anything else as she left.

"What baby? And am I to assume she has something to do with this cuckoo idea of yours?"

She ignored the jab about her idea being cuckoo. "I found an abandoned baby on Friday. Her name is Grace," she told him, and plunged into the story, including what she'd learned from Nina about her chances of keeping the child.

"She's just so precious," she said in conclusion. "If you saw Grace you'd know why I want to keep her. That's why I need to be married. But obviously, I'm not dating anyone seriously so…that's when I thought of you. You're not interested in being married, and besides, we're friends. I couldn't exactly ask a stranger to marry me. Which makes you the perfect person to be in a sham marriage with me."

Tucker had listened intently, only interrupting her to clarify a point or two. The waitress had come and left their food and Maggie was picking at hers, since she'd been too busy talking to eat much. Normally Maggie was good at reading people, it came with her job. But she couldn't tell what Tucker was thinking at all. He just sat there, staring at her with an unblinking gaze.

Tucker rubbed the back of his neck and frowned. "I'm not questioning why you want the baby. But you know it's illegal for CPS to discriminate against you on the basis of your marital status. You don't have to be married to be a foster parent. Or to adopt, for that matter."

"I'm aware of that. But like Nina said, if it comes to a choice between a married couple and a single parent, guess who wins?"

"Legally—" he began.

Frustrated, Maggie interrupted. "It's not about the law, Tucker. We both know that. This is about what really happens. And I can't take the chance that I'd lose her just because I don't happen to have a ring on my finger."

"Maggie, this is insane."

"Please, Tucker." What would she do if he refused her? And if she lost Grace because of that? Pleading wasn't in her nature, but if that's what it took, she'd do it. "It will only be until I can get custody of Grace and for a short time after that. We'll have to stay married for at least a few months, and by then I might know whether I can adopt her. As soon as that's settled we can get a divorce."

"You're nuts, you know that? You're doing all this for a baby you might not even get to keep. Have you thought about what you'll do if the mother shows up?"

"I'll deal with that if and when it happens. In the meantime, Grace needs foster care and I want it to be me. And you, if you'll help me."

"It won't work."

"It will. I know it will work. And it's not like we'll have a real marriage."

"Yeah, about that." He pinned her with a sharp look. "Does this fake marriage have any fringe benefits?"

"What do you mean?"

He arched his brow and smiled. "What do

you think I mean? Does this phony-baloney marriage include sex?"

Stupidly, she hadn't even considered that. She'd been totally focused on her goal of caring for Grace. But now that he mentioned sex, she felt her stomach flutter. She couldn't deny that she'd always wondered what it would be like to go to bed with Tucker. But it would be a mistake. A huge mistake. "No sex," she said decisively. "And no sex with other women, either." No way would she put up with that, fake marriage or not.

"I'm supposed to be celibate for the duration? For what, months? Forget it."

"Cheer up, Tucker. I'll be celibate, too."

"Now I know you're nuts. No, forget it."

But he didn't sound definite to Maggie. She tried another tack. "Marrying me will get your mother off your back. Have you thought about that?"

He seemed struck by the thought and then he started laughing, though he wouldn't tell her why. Maggie had an idea she knew, however.

"I know she doesn't like me but at least if you're married she can't expect you to go out with all the women she's been parading in front of you."

"That part's not really a hardship," Tucker said. "Unless they want to go to the opera."

"I hate opera, too," Maggie said hopefully. "And we do have things in common. We both enjoy Tae Kwon Do and action movies and… well, we've been friends for a long time."

"I don't know. I'd have to be certifiable to agree to this scheme of yours."

He was wavering. She knew it. She could feel it. She put her hand over his. "Don't decide right now. Take some time to think about it." *But not too long.*

"Thinking about it won't make this idea any less insane." He searched her eyes and smiled. "You really want this baby, don't you?"

"More than I've wanted anything in a long time. I can't explain it. She just…something about her calls to me. I have to try."

He sighed. "All right. I'll think about it."

She had to restrain herself from throwing her arms around his neck. "Okay, that's all I ask." He was still regarding her suspiciously, so she added, "Are you busy after lunch?"

"No, why?"

"Come with me to see Grace."

He hesitated for a moment, then shrugged. "All right."

She breathed a sigh of relief. Seeing Grace might not seal the deal, but it couldn't hurt.

Tucker was a nice guy. Surely once he saw Grace and saw how much Maggie wanted to keep her, he'd go along with her plan. And Grace was such a charmer, how could he resist?

BIG MISTAKE, Tucker thought. He'd known it even as he'd agreed to go with Maggie. And now here they were alone with the kid, who he admitted was pretty as could be with her wispy blond curls and dark blue eyes. The foster mother was obviously comfortable with Maggie, because she'd gone off to do laundry or something the minute they showed up. And now Maggie was holding the baby and cooing at her and looking like the complete marshmallow he'd always suspected she was. Tough cop Maggie Barnes was gaga over the kid.

Maggie looked at Tucker and smiled that big, heart-in-her-eyes smile. "Do you want to hold her?"

Hold her? What if he broke her? But he didn't see a way out of it. "I don't know anything about babies," he said without much hope.

"That's all right, I'll show you." She placed the baby in his arms, then stood close by while he held her.

She was so…little. She yawned, blinked at

him with those big blue eyes and waved a tiny fist in the air. A fist the size of a walnut. Good God, how did people take care of anything so fragile and helpless? He made another mistake and looked at Maggie. She met his eyes and smiled again. Damn, she was totally gone over this baby.

"Isn't she precious?" Maggie said, still with the sappy look on her face. And her voice... He'd never heard her sound like that, so tender and, face it, so damn vulnerable. *Vulnerable* wasn't really a word he'd have picked when he thought of Maggie. Until today, that is.

Even Tucker had to admit there was something about the baby that got to him. Something...not needy. More like trusting. "You'd better take her," he said.

Maggie took her back and said, "I'm going to put her down for her nap. We can leave after that."

You're an idiot. You're thinking about doing it. You are actually considering marrying Maggie, he thought as he watched her walk out.

Shortly after that they left and he went back home. But he didn't get a single one of the chores he'd been planning to do accomplished. His house was in a newer subdivision of Aransas City with some fairly substantial homes, though nothing approaching the scale of his parents' waterfront home in Key Allegro. He went out on the deck to sit in the warm February sunshine and think about Maggie's proposal.

He kept seeing Maggie's face when she'd held the baby. She'd looked so happy…and so wistful. Her smile had touched him and the hope in her eyes made him wonder how he could stand to disappoint her.

And they *were* friends. Maybe not as close as they'd been as kids, but he cared about Maggie and had enjoyed renewing the friendship when he'd moved back to town. Still, marrying her seemed a little excessive.

It hit him that he was actually *seriously* considering doing it. She wanted this kid so badly. Otherwise she'd never have proposed such a scheme.

He thought about his parents' reaction and had to grin. His dad would be fine with it, if that's what Tucker wanted. But then his dad had never shared his wife's ambitions for Tucker. His mother would blow a gasket if he told her he was marrying Maggie Barnes. Especially since she'd been pushing Isabella at him as hard as she could.

Maggie was a cop and the daughter of a fisherman, not the sort of woman his mother had dreamed of him marrying. Maggie had no patience for the social scene or any of the other things Eileen Jones held near and dear. And while Tucker loved his mother, he had to admit, one of her major faults was that she was a snob. Cops and fishermen were not genteel, not in Eileen Jones's world.

If he did marry Maggie, he'd have to come down hard on his mother. He wouldn't allow her to disrespect his bride, even if she was a fake bride.

But could he live with Maggie and not have sex? Wouldn't that be too weird?

Tucker spent the rest of the afternoon and evening thinking. By the next afternoon, he knew he wouldn't get anything accomplished until he'd taken care of the problem.

He called Maggie's home and got no answer, then tracked her down at work. "When are you off?"

"My shift's over in an hour. I came in early today. Have you decided?"

He didn't answer that directly. "We need to talk. I'll come to your house after your shift."

"All right. I'll see you then."

He'd made his decision. Now all he had to do was convince Maggie to change the game plan. Not in a major way. Just one little detail.

TUCKER WAS WAITING for Maggie on her front porch when she came home so she went in that way instead of through the kitchen as she usually did. She hadn't been able to tell on the phone, but she suspected he was going to turn her down. So she'd spent the rest of her shift trying to brace for it.

"Hey, Tucker."

"Hey, Maggie."

He followed her in and she tossed her keys down on the hall table. She hung the jacket she hadn't needed on the hook by the door. Walking into the living room, she took her Glock out, checked it, then laid it on the coffee table. Next came the equipment belt, which went on the table beside the Glock.

If she ever did get to keep Grace she'd have to lock up her weapon. That would be one of the first things CPS made sure of. She stretched and wished she'd had time to have a little workout with the punching bag before Tucker arrived. It might have relaxed her.

"What?" she asked because Tucker was staring at her.

He grinned. "I've never seen you take off your cop stuff before. It's kind of…sexy."

Maggie laughed. "Right. Are you hitting on me, Tucker?"

"Well, that's what I came to talk to you about. That and your proposal."

"You decided not to, didn't you?"

"No, I decided I'd marry you."

She stared at him. "Really?" Her heart thudded painfully. He wouldn't joke about that, would he?

He stuck his hands in his pockets and walked away a few steps. "I'll marry you but I'm not sure about one of your conditions."

"What condition is that?" she asked warily.

"I don't think we can live together and pretend to be married and never have sex. It just won't work, Maggie."

"You're saying if I want to marry you I have to have sex with you. That's blackmail."

"Don't be ridiculous. And that's not what I said, exactly. I said it wouldn't work."

"Sex would be a mistake. Think how messy it would be once we divorced."

"I don't see why. If we both know going in this is temporary, why shouldn't we enjoy ourselves?"

She was appalled to discover she was considering it, and not simply because she wanted to be married. "You don't really want to sleep with me, Tucker. You just don't want to be celibate for months."

He walked over to her, reached out and gently played with her hair. "You're wrong about that, Maggie." He paused and added, "Did you know I had a thing for you in high school?"

"Liar," she said a little breathlessly. She was finding it hard to breathe. The man had no right to be so gorgeous. And when he smiled at her like he was doing now… Oh, baby. What had ever made her think Tucker Jones would be safe? That she could marry him and not want to sleep with him? Stupidity, that's what. Still, she hadn't come this far to give up now.

"Yeah, you had a thing for me all right. Is that why you stood me up for the homecoming dance?"

He frowned. "I knew you still held that against me. I was eighteen and stupid, Maggie."

"You were a slime," she stated categorically, moving away from him. "You stood me up because Annette Carson said she'd sleep with you if you took her instead of me." At least, that was the story she'd heard. She'd never found out if it was truth or rumor. But judging by Tucker's expression, it held more than a grain of truth. "I cried about you, you jerk."

He winced at that. "I didn't sleep with her," he said. "And I knew I'd made a mistake as soon as I did it. You never gave me another chance after that."

"Once burned, you know. But it doesn't matter now, anyway."

"Doesn't it? Would it help if I told you I regretted it ever since I did it?"

"Huh. Because she wouldn't put out, I imagine."

"No, because I hurt you and you never forgave me."

"I forgave you. We were still friends after that."

He laughed. "After you made me grovel. Yeah, I guess we were friends."

"You have a point," she conceded. "Living together and not having sex might not be easy, but we're both adults. We should be able to put our glands on hold if necessary."

"That's just it. Why is it necessary?"

Part of her wished it wasn't. But she had to be realistic. "Because sex would make the marriage too real. And neither one of us is ready for that."

He didn't look convinced. He'd put his hands in his pockets and was studying her. He still wore his office clothes, tailored khaki slacks and a powder-blue dress shirt with the sleeves rolled up over muscular forearms. Her mouth went a little dry just looking at him. She wondered why she didn't simply agree and make it easy on both of them.

"Admit it, Tucker. You don't want a real marriage any more than I do. Sex would complicate everything."

"Maggie—"

She broke in before he could shoot her down. "There's another reason. I'm not cut out for meaningless sex."

"This might come as a shock to you, but I don't much care for it, either. But I don't think making love to you would be meaningless, Maggie."

"That's as much of a problem as if it *were* meaningless. What if one of us fell for the other? That would bring nothing but pain to both of us."

"I don't know." He shook his head. "I see what you're saying, but that doesn't change the facts."

Her heart sank. He was trying to let her down gently. Maybe he was right. A fake marriage was too much to expect from him. But she wanted Grace so badly she'd been willing to try anything to get her. Almost anything. She knew herself too well, though. If she went to bed with Tucker, she'd fall for him. And she couldn't risk that. "What facts?" she asked, clamping down on her emotions.

"We're going to have to pretend to an intimacy we haven't experienced. It won't be easy."

"No, but we can do it. I know we can."

As he looked at her a rueful smile twisted his lips. "I care about you, Maggie."

Hope burgeoned. "I know. I care about you, too. What are you saying?"

"What the hell. I'll marry you."

"Really?" She wanted to throw her arms around him but she restrained herself. "Marriage and no sex?"

"If that's the way you want it."

"I think that's best for both of us, considering the circumstances." She held out a hand. "Shake on it?"

Tucker looked at her hand, then at her face and smiled. "Don't you think we should seal this deal with a kiss?" He took her hand and tugged her closer.

His mouth curved upward, his eyes were smiling, but there was understanding in them, too. She hesitated, torn between doing what she wanted and doing the smart thing. But damn it, a woman didn't get engaged every day. Sham or not, she was still talking about marriage.

"You don't want our first kiss to be at the wedding when the preacher says 'you may now kiss the bride,' do you?"

"That would definitely be safer," she said, and he laughed.

He pulled her closer, their joined hands pinned between them. She slid one hand up his arm and around his neck. His other arm came around her to hold her lightly at the waist. Maggie was a tall woman but Tucker was several inches taller than her and she had to look up to see his face.

"Are you sure about this, Tucker?"

"About kissing you?"

"No, about the whole thing."

He smiled and his arm tightened around her. "Let's get married," he said softly, and then he kissed her.

CHAPTER FIVE

HE'D ONLY MEANT IT as a friendly kiss. But her lips were soft, and tempting, and when he traced the bow with his tongue, they parted and welcomed him inside. She tasted sweet, and a little spicy, and exactly as he'd always imagined Maggie would taste.

Damn. *Friends,* he reminded himself. He turned her loose and smiled.

She returned his smile with a saucy one of her own, and said, "Now why am I not surprised you're good at that?"

He laughed. Obviously, she hadn't been as affected as he had. It would be good to remember that. "You're not so bad yourself."

She gave him a cheeky grin. "I guess we need to talk about details. I'd like to do this as soon as possible. How long is the waiting period after you get a marriage license?"

"Three days. I looked it up before I came

over." He checked his watch. "We still have time to go to the courthouse today and apply for it. Then we can get married on Friday. Are you going to talk to your minister?"

"I don't know, Tucker." She frowned and rubbed her arm. "I'd feel like a hypocrite if I asked my pastor to marry us. Let's just go down to the justice of the peace and do it at his office."

That would be logical, he supposed. But if they wanted people to take them seriously, he thought a traditional wedding would be best. Still, for now, he held his tongue. "We can talk about those details later. Right now we should go apply for the license."

"Okay, let me change." She picked up her gun and equipment belt and took them with her.

Maggie came back a short time later in jeans and a lightweight sea-green sweater that turned her hazel eyes a soft, mossy green. She'd brushed her hair and left it down. Her hair was an amazing mix of colors. Everything from deep auburn to strands of strawberry blond. It was soft, too, as he'd discovered earlier. He controlled an impulse to touch it again, and decided not to think about what it would feel like against his bare skin. Much better not think about that, since it wasn't going to happen.

"I'll drive," he said. "We need to go buy you a ring after we go to the courthouse."

Maggie looked at him in surprise as they walked out the door. "You mean an engagement ring? I don't need one. All I need is a plain wedding band."

He opened the Mustang's door and let her in, then got in himself before he answered. "If you're marrying me you need an engagement ring." He started the car and pulled away from the curb.

"I don't see why. It's just a needless expense."

He shot her an amused glance. "Maggie, do you want everyone to believe this marriage is for real?"

"Of course. That's the only way to make sure the CPS doesn't get wind of the truth."

"Then you need an engagement ring. No one who knows me will believe I didn't buy my fiancée a ring."

She grumbled but she conceded his point. He had a feeling they weren't through arguing about the ring and knew he was right an hour later when they walked into a jewelry store in Corpus Christi.

Maggie strode in, every inch the officer in control. He regarded her with some amusement as she looked at the case the clerk pointed out and immediately zeroed in on a ring with a diamond so tiny he needed a magnifying glass to see it.

"This one looks good," Maggie said, pointing. "How much is it?"

The clerk looked disappointed and Tucker couldn't blame her. He caught the woman's eye and shook his head. "My fiancée is being thrifty, but I'm not." He gestured to another ring, a simple solitaire setting but with a decent-size diamond. It looked like Maggie, he thought. "Let us see that one."

"That's a lovely choice, sir." The clerk beamed.

"Tucker, that's too expensive."

He noticed the mutinous set to her jaw and smiled. "Excuse us a minute," he told the clerk and, putting his hand under her arm, led Maggie outside. She started arguing the moment they walked out the door. Leaning back against the planter in the center of the courtyard, he let her rant. Patiently, he waited as she made her case, which consisted mainly of her arguing that she didn't think a hunk of glass should cost so much and she didn't intend to pay for something so ridiculously outrageous.

"Are you through?"

"I guess." Her eyes flashed with annoyance. He didn't bother to debate, but gave her the clincher to his case. "Maggie, if you get that dinky little ring everyone in town will know the marriage is fake."

"Why should they? No one will notice."

"Who are you kidding? We're living in Aransas City, gossip capital of the U.S. Besides, my parents would know the instant they saw it. You don't want them to know our real reason for getting married, do you?"

"No, of course I don't." She sulked. "If you didn't have so much money it wouldn't be a problem."

Tucker laughed out loud at that. "You really are one in a million. You're the only woman I know who's unhappy because her fiancé has money. Let me buy the ring for you."

"We'll split it," she announced. "And all the other expenses, too."

She couldn't afford half of what that ring cost. Not on a cop's salary. Besides, he wanted to buy it for her. "Nope. I buy the ring."

"Tucker—"

"It's a deal breaker. Take it or leave it." She glared at him. "Are you armed?" he asked. If that was the way she looked at suspects, he was glad he wasn't one.

"Always."

That surprised him. "You wear your weapon to the jewelry store?"

"My Glock is with me whenever I'm dressed." She reached behind her back and said, "It's either here or, if I can't conceal it, I have a purse with a hidden holster. I'm a cop. If I see a crime being committed I'm expected to intervene. Why do you ask?"

He hadn't known that, but then, he'd never dated a cop before. Or been engaged to one. And not being a criminal lawyer, he didn't know a lot of cops well. "Because you looked like you were about to blow me away."

"Ha-ha. No, I save that for the bad guys. You're merely annoying." She paced away from him a step, then turned back. "It's not right, Tucker. I don't want you spending your money on me. This marriage thing was all my idea."

"Yes, but I agreed to it. So we need to do it right. There's no point in our getting married if we announce to the world it's fake."

"I guess you're right," she said grudgingly. "You can always sell it once we're divorced."

As if he would take the ring back from her. Not a chance in hell. But wisely, he kept his thoughts to himself.

They went back inside and walked out with

the engagement ring Tucker had chosen and two plain gold wedding bands that he decided he'd better let her have her way about. Maggie stated categorically that she wouldn't wear "the rock," as she referred to it, to work. She wanted something plain, that she felt comfortable with. Something that if she lost or damaged, she wouldn't have a heart attack over. So he gave in.

There would be other arguments, he felt sure. But he'd won the battle of the engagement ring. Oddly enough, he found he liked seeing his ring on her finger. Maybe this marriage wasn't as bizarre of an idea as he'd thought at first.

Surreptitiously, Maggie looked at her left hand. The diamond sparkled, even in the dim, romantic lighting of the classy seafood restaurant Tucker had suggested they go to, to eat and discuss the rest of the wedding plans.

Tucker had told the clerk to put the ring in a small velvet box, then insisted Maggie let him slide the rock on her finger once they went back to his car. She'd been a little afraid that he'd kiss her. He hadn't, but instead of being relieved he'd acquiesced to her wishes, she was conscious of a vague feeling of disappointment.

The rock was gorgeous, the kind of ring any

woman would kill for. A ring totally unsuited to a hardworking, firmly middle-class cop. Maggie had never felt more guilty in her life.

She shot him an irritated glance. Damn it, why couldn't he have been poor? Or at least middle class, like her? "I didn't ask you to marry me because you're loaded, you know."

Tucker looked up from the wine list he was studying and smiled. "I know. I wouldn't have agreed to marry you if I thought you were after me for my money."

The waiter came back and Tucker ordered a bottle of wine for them. White, because that's what she liked. Maggie had a feeling he wouldn't let her pay for half of dinner, either. "Is that why you haven't ever married? Because you think women are after your money?"

"I don't think all of them are. But I know for a fact at least one was."

"Sounds like there's a story there."

The waiter had returned and Tucker let him open the wine, pour out a taste and then, when he nodded, pour them both a glass. He took another sip of wine and set his glass down. Maggie sipped hers and sighed. Whatever it was, it tasted like liquid gold.

He smiled cynically. "Yeah, there's a story."

"You don't want to talk about it."

"Maybe some other time. Right now I think our time would be better spent talking about the wedding. We need to tell both our parents, obviously. Do you think your parents will want to have the wedding at their house?"

Maggie didn't have to think long about that. "No. They had my sister's wedding at the house and my mother swore never again. She was a nervous wreck and the house was in shambles afterward. On top of that, somebody's kid broke the TV and my dad was so angry he didn't speak to Lorna for a month. Let's just go down to the JP."

"I have a better idea. We'll have the wedding and reception at my parents' house."

Maggie goggled at him. "Are you insane? Have the wedding at the mansion?" She remembered his parents' home from high school, when Tucker had parties.

"It's not a mansion."

"In my book it is. Your mother will freak. She's going to freak anyway, isn't she?"

"They'll be surprised. But they'll deal with it. Don't worry, I'll handle my parents. We'll tell both sets of parents tomorrow night. We can plan the wedding and reception with my parents then."

She started to argue but he wore the same determined expression as when he'd decided to give her the rock. Damn, the man could be stubborn. "Okay, if it's all right with your folks we can have the wedding there, but there's no need for a reception. Aren't we just having family?"

"Family and a few friends. It won't be large. There's not enough time. We'll just call a few of our friends and ask them. I want to ask my partner and his wife and my secretary and her husband. You'll want to ask your chief and his wife, I'm sure. And whoever else you work with that you want to come. We can make out the list tonight when we get back."

Her head was whirling. She hadn't realized everything would be so complicated. She hadn't thought things through at all. For a smart woman she was starting to realize she'd been incredibly dumb about this whole thing. Fortunately, the waiter came back and took their order, which gave her a little time to compose herself.

She changed the subject. "Do you want to come see Grace with me tomorrow? I have a meeting set up in the morning and I thought you might want to be there, too."

"Sure. Let me know what time and I'll

arrange my schedule. Have you made any headway locating her mother?"

"No, not yet. So far every lead has fizzled. The woman could be anywhere by now. She's gone underground and it's hard to find them when they do that." Guiltily, Maggie acknowledged that she didn't want the cops to find the mother. Grace deserved better than a mother who had abandoned her.

"When do we start the process for applying to be foster parents?"

"I have some of the paperwork, which I've already started on, but I do need your input on some of it. We have to take a course they call pre-training, to certify us in child care. Then they'll want a caseworker to come out and assess us, and our home. I have a long list of the kind of questions they ask. It's pretty intense."

It occurred to her she hadn't thought their living arrangements through, either. "Do you mind moving into my house?" She looked at him and her heart sank. He just smiled and shook his head.

"Afraid not, Maggie. You're going to have to move in with me."

"Why? Because your house is bigger?"

"Partly. It just makes sense to live in the newer house."

Newer, bigger and nicer, she thought, but she didn't say it. "I'm not selling my house. I like my house. Besides, I'll need it after we get divorced."

"I agree, there's no need to sell it. Why don't you just rent it out?"

She could do that easily enough. Rentals were scarce in Aransas City so they rented out almost immediately whenever one came up.

The waiter brought their salads. They ate in silence for a moment and then Tucker said, "Where do you want to go on our honeymoon?"

Honeymoon? "Oh, no," she said, laying down her fork. "No way. I gave in on the ring. I gave in on where we have the wedding. I even gave in on the house. I've given in on every damn thing you've mentioned. But we are not going on a honeymoon. Absolutely not."

He gave her a pitying look. "Yeah, babe, we are."

"Stop calling me 'babe.' It's annoying. Read my lips. No honeymoon."

Tucker put down his fork and looked at her with exasperation. "You're not being logical, Maggie. If we're getting married because we're in love—which, I have to remind you, is what we want everyone to think—then we'd want to take a honeymoon. It doesn't have to be long, just a few days. Are you working this weekend?"

"No." She snapped the word out, along with a death look.

"Good. Then ask your chief for a few more days off and we'll go on a honeymoon."

The waiter cleared their salad plates. "Your main course will be right out," he said, and poured more wine.

Maggie gulped some and glared at Tucker. Why had she never realized what a control freak he was? If he thought he was calling all the shots in this phony marriage, he had another think coming.

Preferring to brood in silence, she waited until the waiter had set their main course in front of them before she spoke again.

"We're not in love. In fact, I don't even like you right now."

Tucker laughed. "You're just mad because I'm right. Why don't we go skiing? Have you ever been?"

Maggie took another drink of her wine and tossed her hair over her shoulder with a twist of her head. "Oh, sure. I go to Switzerland every year and ski the Alps."

His lips curved. "Switzerland's too far. I like

Steamboat Springs, Colorado. We can fly into Dallas Friday night and there's a direct flight out the next morning. I'll see if I can get us in at the condo where I usually stay. Failing that, my partner has a second home there and I don't think they're using it this weekend."

"I don't have any ski clothes. And I don't have time to buy them."

"Don't worry about it. My partner's wife is about your size. I'm sure she'll lend you whatever you need. And then we'll rent equipment for you there. You'll like it, you'll see. You're athletic, so I'm sure you'll pick it up quickly."

Maggie leaned forward and pinned him with the look she usually reserved for low-life scumbags she interrogated. "You're insane. Completely insane."

He laughed again. "Loosen up, Maggie. It'll be fun."

Fun? A romantic honeymoon with Tucker, the very appealing man she'd sworn not to go to bed with. What had she gotten herself into? And what had she dragged Tucker into?

"Tucker?" He looked up from his plate and smiled at her. "Maybe we shouldn't do this."

"Cold feet, Maggie?"

"Frozen. I hadn't realized it would be so com-

plicated. I didn't think things through very well."
She shook her head. "This is so not like me."

Tucker covered her hand with his. Her left
hand, the one wearing the ring he'd insisted on
buying her. "You've been focused on your goal.
You want the baby, don't you?"

"You know I do."

"And you believe your chances of getting
to keep her will be much better if we're
married, right?"

"Yes, but—"

"Then let's get married. Maggie," he said,
squeezing her hand gently. "I wouldn't do this
if I didn't want to."

She stared at him for a long moment, then
smiled reluctantly. "Okay. But I hope you don't
regret it."

"I won't. And I don't think you will, either."

Maggie shook off her uneasiness. Focus on
the goal, she thought. Keeping Grace. And don't
think about the possibility that marriage with
Tucker Jones might be nothing like she
expected when she'd first proposed.

CHAPTER SIX

"CAN I GET YOU something to drink?" Colleen Barnes asked late the next afternoon after she'd shown Tucker and Maggie into the living room. "Tea or something stronger?"

She looked a little bewildered, Maggie thought. And why shouldn't she since Maggie hadn't told her parents anything beyond she was bringing someone to see them. She'd kept the ring hidden, so she wouldn't have to explain immediately, but maybe that had been a mistake.

"No, thanks, Mom. We can't stay long." They had to face the dragon lady next, which was her private name for Tucker's mother. She knew she ought to be past it by now, but Eileen Jones had always intimidated her. It didn't matter that Maggie was a grown woman and a cop to boot, Eileen could make her feel like an unsophisticated kid with one condescending look. The last time she'd pulled the woman over for speeding came to mind.

"Frank, turn that TV off, you hear? Maggie wants to talk to us."

Maggie's father looked irritated but he muted the TV. It was tuned to his favorite station, the Fishing Channel. "What in Sam Hill is this about, Maggie? You've never brought a man over here before. Not since you've been grown, anyway."

She shot a glance at Tucker, who was clearly struggling not to laugh. Great, her father was grumpy and her mother bewildered. She should have told them by herself. She decided just to get it over with. She thrust out her left hand to show them the rock. "I'm getting married. This Friday."

"Huh." Frank glanced at the ring, then sent Tucker a speculative look. "You don't say."

"Married?" her mother repeated blankly, staring at Maggie's hand. "To Tucker?"

Tucker took her right hand and squeezed it. She didn't dare look at him because they'd both burst out laughing. "Of course, to Tucker. Why else would I bring him?"

"Isn't this kind of sudden?" Colleen said, looking from one to the other. "We didn't even know you were dating anyone, Maggie."

"Say what you mean, Colleen." Her father looked at Tucker. "Is she pregnant?"

"Not to my knowledge," Tucker said.

Maggie squeezed his hand, hard. "Of course I'm not pregnant."

"I've been asking Maggie to marry me since I moved back to the area," Tucker announced, as if he wasn't speaking a bald-faced lie. "Yesterday she finally said yes."

"And we decided there's no reason to wait," Maggie said hastily. They had discussed what their story would be, but now that Maggie heard it spoken out loud she thought it sounded lame. Oh, well, she thought, that couldn't be helped now. "So we're getting married this Friday. At Tucker's parents' house. I'll let you know the details later." Unless his mother flipped out and they had to change plans. They should have eloped. Gone to Vegas and tied the knot there. Too late now, they'd chosen their course.

"Do you have a dress, honey?"

Maggie smiled at her mother. "Not yet. Will you go with me to look tomorrow? I'm working the morning shift, but we can go tomorrow afternoon."

"I'd love to. I'll make a list of bridal shops."

"It's informal. I want a short dress, so we can just go to a regular shop."

"Bridal shops have short dresses, Maggie."

The dress was the least of her worries. "Whatever, we'll decide tomorrow." She got up, pulling Tucker with her. "What's wrong, Dad?"

Frank frowned at both of them and rubbed his jaw. "Do I have to wear a suit?"

"Of course you have to wear a suit. You wore a suit to Lorna's wedding and didn't complain."

"Yes, he did," her mother said.

"Don't fit anymore." He sighed heavily. "I guess I could see if my burying suit fits."

She looked at Tucker and had to bite her lip. Great. Her dad was wearing his funeral suit to her wedding. Not a good omen, that.

They barely made it to the car before they both burst out laughing. "Oh, my God," Maggie finally said, wiping her eyes. "I don't know how I kept a straight face."

"It was tough," Tucker agreed as he started the car. "I was doing okay until the part about the burying suit. And his expression when he said it was priceless."

"At least that's over with," Maggie said.

"One set down, one to go."

Yeah, the ones she was worried about. "What if your mom freaks out?"

"She's not going to freak out. That's the third time you've said that. Why are you so nervous?"

"I'm not nervous." Terrified, maybe. She pulled out her cell phone and said, "Oh, look. The chief called when I had the ringer silenced. I'm sure he needs me to come in."

Tucker's glance was chock full of disbelief. "Liar. Good God, Maggie, you're a cop. You face down armed criminals. Telling my parents we're getting married should be a walk in the park to you."

"Huh. I'll take the criminal any day. I know what to do with them. I don't have a clue how to deal with your mother. I can't exactly throw her in jail because she makes me nervous."

Tucker laughed. "Cheer up. She's not as bad as you think."

Wanna bet? she thought. A short while later they pulled up to the mansion. It looked just like Maggie remembered. Big. Imposing. She glanced at Tucker, who was smiling at her. "Let's get this over with," she said.

"Okay." But he didn't get out. He simply looked at her, focusing on…her mouth. He was staring at her mouth and unless she mistook that gleam in his eyes… Oh, God, he was going to kiss her. And damn if she didn't want him to.

But he didn't. He dropped his gaze and said, "Let's go."

She'd imagined it, she thought, feeling foolish. They'd agreed they wouldn't have sex, so why would he kiss her? And why was she so disappointed that he hadn't?

"MOM, DAD, YOU REMEMBER Maggie Barnes, don't you?" Tucker said as they followed his father into the living room. Since Tucker had told his mother he was bringing someone with him, she had set out a tray of canapés, arranged almost perfectly on the antique silver platter she used to impress company. Someone—his dad, he was sure—had already eaten a couple, marring the perfect symmetry and no doubt incurring his mother's censure.

"Certainly. I hope you're not in trouble with the law, darling," she said with a laugh. She sat in one of the side chairs and sipped her wine.

His father offered Maggie a hand. "Harvey Jones. It's been a long time. Basketball, right? You were captain of the girls' team in high school."

Maggie smiled as she shook hands with

him. "That's right. I can't believe you remembered that."

"I like sports," Harvey said. "Watched a lot of the games when Tucker was in school, although football was always Tucker's game. What can I get you to drink?"

"Maggie will have white wine and I'll take a beer."

"Coming right up," he said, and stepped behind the bar. "What's this about Tucker being in trouble with the law, Eileen? Am I missing a joke?"

His mother had caught sight of Maggie's left hand and was staring at it with a fascinated and, he admitted, slightly sour expression. "Maggie's a policewoman in Aransas City," she said.

"Are you, now?" He handed Maggie her wine and Tucker his beer. "Now that's an interesting career."

"Obviously, she hasn't stopped you for speeding or you'd know that, Harvey," his mother said waspishly.

Maggie rolled her eyes at Tucker. He grinned back.

"Well, Tucker, what is this about?" Eileen asked. "I had to cancel my meeting with the opera committee since you were so insistent on my being here."

"I think my news is a little more interesting than your opera committee." He reached for Maggie's hand. "Maggie and I are getting married this Friday. We wanted to talk to you about having the wedding here. And the reception, of course."

His mother choked on her wine. His father shot him a keen glance, then said, "Congratulations, son." He shook hands with Tucker and when Maggie offered hers, he smiled and took it, then bent to kiss her cheek. "Congratulations, my dear. His mother and I happen to think Tucker's pretty special."

"Thank you. So do I," Maggie said, surprising him.

"Married?" Eileen said faintly. "You and— and— You and *Maggie* are getting married?"

"Show her the rock," Tucker said to Maggie.

"Tucker." Maggie gave him a warning glance before turning back to his mother and smiling down at her a little anxiously. "I know it's kind of a shock."

Eileen stared at Maggie, then patted her lips with a napkin. "Yes, you might say that. I wasn't aware you and Maggie were even seeing each other, Tucker," she said, her voice having regained its strength. "This is very sudden, isn't it? Is there a particular reason you're in such a rush?"

"Relax, Mom. Maggie's not pregnant."

Maggie kicked him.

"Ouch." He rubbed his shin and grinned at Maggie, whose eyes were dark green and flashing him death threats. "I was only saying what she was thinking."

"Really, Tucker, that was uncalled for," Eileen said. "I thought no such thing. I simply wondered why I had heard nothing of this."

"Why don't we sit down and talk about it?" Harvey asked. Tucker and Maggie sat on the couch while his dad took the other side chair.

Tucker took Maggie's hand again and told his parents the same thing he'd told Maggie's parents. "I've been asking Maggie to marry me for almost a year now. Since shortly after I moved to Aransas City and we got to know each other again. It took me this long to convince her to marry me. I'm not waiting for her to change her mind."

Neither of them looked as if they were buying that lie. But neither Maggie nor Tucker could think of a better one, other than that Maggie was pregnant and they'd already blown that one by telling her parents she wasn't.

"If Maggie isn't certain about the wedding perhaps you should wait," Eileen said, looking hopeful.

"Well, Maggie? What do you say?" He tilted his head and considered her.

Her lips curved as she looked at him. "I'm sure. What about you?"

"Absolutely." Since it seemed necessary, he kissed her lightly.

"Sounds like we're having a wedding, Eileen."

"Yes, it does."

She sounded resigned. Maybe she wouldn't be as difficult as he'd thought.

"This Friday?" Eileen repeated. "And you want to have the wedding here? At our house?"

"That was Tucker's idea," Maggie said hastily. "It's no problem if we can't. We'll just go down to the justice of the peace's office."

Tucker nearly laughed. She couldn't have said anything more calculated to give his mother palpitations. Harvey and Eileen Jones's only offspring getting married at the JP's office?

Eileen gave a faint moan. "No, no. If you insist on getting married in this—this rushed fashion, you'll have it here."

"Thank you."

"How many people are you inviting?"

"No more than fifty. Maybe not that many."

"Definitely not that many," Maggie said,

sending him a severe glare. "We just want family and a few friends."

His dad hadn't said much. He was still watching them closely, though. Sometimes Tucker wished his old man wasn't so observant.

"About the decorations, the flowers and such, do you have a theme in mind?" Eileen asked Maggie.

Maggie threw him a panicked glance. "Theme?"

"We just decided this yesterday, Mom. Maggie hasn't had time to think about all that."

She waved him aside. "Nonsense. Maggie's close to your age, isn't she? Surely she's thought about what she wants her wedding to be like. Haven't you?"

"Not exactly," Maggie said.

"Is this your first marriage?"

"Yes. Why?"

"Just curious, dear." She laughed again. "I can't imagine not having thought about my wedding at your age. Why, I had mine planned from the time I was fourteen."

"Tucker, would you mind looking at something for me?" Harvey said. "In my office."

"Sure, Dad." He hated to leave Maggie but his mother seemed to be behaving herself and

Maggie was doing all right. "I'll be back in a minute," he told her.

"Take your time," Eileen said. "Maggie and I will get all these details ironed out."

Tucker followed his dad to his office. Harvey shut the door and said, "I don't have anything to show you. I just wanted to ask you what's going on."

"I'm getting married. I thought it was pretty self-explanatory."

Harvey crossed his arms and leaned back against the edge of his desk. "Not this time. You're not in love with Maggie, Tucker. And you said she wasn't pregnant. So I have to ask, why are you marrying her?"

Crap. He should have known his father would see through the lie. He wanted to tell him the truth, but he'd promised Maggie. Besides, he wasn't entirely sure his father wouldn't let it slip to his mother. And if she knew, that would be a disaster.

"You're wrong, Dad. I've been in love with Maggie for months."

"Which is why you've been dating a number of other women all this time," he said drily. "Including, your mother tells me, Isabella Jensen. Your mother thought you were serious about her."

"No, not at all. I told you Maggie wouldn't marry me. I was trying to forget about her." Tucker figured the less said about other women, the better. "I want to marry Maggie. I'm thirty-five, Dad, I know what I'm doing."

"You should, but I'm not sure that you do." He considered Tucker a moment, then smiled. "She's a beautiful woman. Unusual."

"Yeah." Tucker smiled, too. "Maggie's one in a million."

"Well, as you pointed out, you're a grown man. Let's go rescue your bride-to-be from your mother."

Tucker laughed. "Mom seemed to take the news pretty well. Better than I'd expected."

Harvey laid a hand on his shoulder. "With your mother you can never tell. I wouldn't be too complacent."

"Maggie's a cop. I'd back her against Mom anytime."

ARMED ROBBERS. Murderers. Thugs. Bangers. Psychos. Oh, why couldn't the chief call and tell her he had an emergency? Anything would be better than being interrogated by the dragon lady, Maggie thought.

That nice, slightly puzzled demeanor she'd

displayed while Tucker was in the room had vanished the instant he left. She'd begun firing questions at Maggie like a general marshaling his troops. Oh, she hadn't been overtly rude, but it was clear from her questions that she thought Maggie was a damn poor choice as a bride for her precious son. Her attitude annoyed Maggie but she felt guilty, too. Eileen Jones only wanted the best for Tucker and she had no idea this so-called marriage was a sham.

"So we're agreed on white roses?"

"That's fine. I really don't want you to go to a lot of trouble, Mrs. Jones. I told Tucker we could—"

"Please." She raised a hand with a look of revulsion. "Don't mention the justice of the peace again. My son will not be married in an office."

Maggie bit her tongue. Eileen had pulled out paper and pen and started making a list. "Now, about the food. Did you have anything special in mind?"

Maggie looked at her blankly. She had no idea what to serve at a wedding reception. "I'm sure my mother could bring something. She loves to cook." Unlike Maggie, who considered it torture.

Eileen looked up from her list. "Home cooking?" She laughed, that short, high-pitched tinkle that made Maggie long for earplugs. "Really, Maggie, I hardly think that will be necessary. We'll have it catered. I'm sure I can find someone who'll help out on the spur of the moment."

Maggie fidgeted. "Have it catered? Won't that be expensive?"

"Expensive? What has that got to do with it?" She looked as if she'd never heard of the concept.

"I thought all this was the bride's responsibility." Maggie gestured to include the huge room. "You know, the reception and all that."

"Yes, I suppose it is. Traditionally. But yours is hardly a traditional wedding, now, is it?" She gave her a superior smile. "Don't worry, dear. We'll take care of it. I'm sure you can't afford this sort of thing on the salary of a *public servant*." She said the last two words with an audible sneer.

That fired Maggie's temper. *You're a cop,* she thought. *Where are your ovaries?* She stood. "Thanks, but no thanks. I'm paying for the reception. I'll order the flowers. And my mother can be in charge of the food. Tucker and I will deal with the drinks, too." She entertained a brief, but satisfying, image of a keg of beer smack in the middle of Eileen's elegant white living room. "You won't have to worry about anything except to tell people where to put things."

Tucker and his father came back into the room just then. Irrationally, Maggie wanted to kick Tucker. She contented herself with glaring at him instead.

"What's going on?" Tucker said.

"Why nothing, darling," his mother replied, unperturbed by Maggie's statement. "Maggie here is insisting on paying for the reception and arranging everything herself. I had merely offered her my assistance, but she obviously doesn't want my help." She sniffed, clearly offended.

Maggie gritted her teeth. She wasn't backing down on this one and if Tucker thought she would he could kiss her lily-white—

"We'll talk it over and let you know tomorrow, Mom. We need to get going. Maggie has the early shift in the morning."

Harvey gave her another kiss on the cheek before they left. Maggie really liked Tucker's father. But his mother was going to take some getting used to. It was a very good thing that the marriage was only temporary. Otherwise Maggie would have to face a lifetime of being detested by her mother-in-law.

CHAPTER SEVEN

IT TOOK MOST OF the next morning for Maggie to fill out a report on a cow that liked to walk through town and drop cow patties along Main Street. She'd cited the owner repeatedly, but because the man had known her since she was in diapers, he didn't pay much attention to her. With long practice, Maggie ignored the almost continually ringing phones until Dottie, the receptionist, buzzed her.

She picked up the receiver, cradling it on her shoulder as she typed. "Officer Barnes."

"Maggie, dear, this is Eileen."

For a minute she drew a blank. "Hello, Mrs. Jones. What can I do for you?"

"I'd like to take you to lunch, if you're free. We can discuss some details about the wedding."

"I don't think Tucker—"

"Oh, no, just us girls. Why don't you come to the country club, around one?"

Oh, right. In my uniform? They'd faint. Glad for the excuse, she said, "I'm sorry, I only have a short lunch hour. Maybe we should try another—"

Again, she was interrupted before she finished her sentence. "Then I'll come to you. Where do you suggest we meet?"

Why had she even mentioned having a lunch hour? Trapped, Maggie said, "We have a decent Mexican place and the Scarlet Parrot bar and grill. Oh, and there's a pretty good burger place." Which she could not see Eileen Jones going to, but it gave them another choice.

"I've eaten at the Scarlet Parrot with Tucker before. Let's go there."

"All right, I'll see you at one." Something told her she was not going to enjoy this lunch. But maybe that was just her suspicious mind. Maybe Mrs. Jones just wanted to get to know Maggie better. How bad could it be?

NATURALLY, she was late. Only by about ten minutes, but still, not the best way to impress your future mother-in-law.

"Maggie, hi," Delilah said when she walked in. "Are you alone?"

"Ah, no. I'm meeting someone." She

looked around, spying Eileen by the windows. "There she is."

Delilah turned in the direction Maggie was looking as Eileen waved. "Isn't that Tucker's mother?"

"Um, yes."

"And you and Tucker were just here the other day."

"Uh, yes," she said again.

Delilah raised a brow and said, "Really. I know there's a story here."

Oh, for God's sake, Maggie thought, feeling her face heat. *I'm blushing and I never blush.* "I'll tell you about it later. I'm late." She hurried over to Eileen's table. "Sorry for keeping you waiting. I got tied up at work."

"That's quite all right, dear. Think nothing of it."

Maggie relaxed marginally after they ordered drinks and food. Eileen seemed to be going out of her way to put Maggie at ease, chatting away about nothing in particular. So why did she get the feeling that a Mack truck was about to hit her dead between the eyes?

The feeling persisted as their food was served. Maggie took a bite of shrimp, washed it down with a sip of tea, then said, "Was there something in particular you wanted to talk about? I mean, about the wedding details?"

Eileen had taken a bite of her shrimp salad and looked pleasantly surprised. "This is quite good."

"Best on the coast," Maggie said with pride, as if she owned the restaurant herself. "The owner and his wife are good friends of mine."

"Hmm. Yes, now about the wedding." She leaned forward and smiled, but it wasn't sweet. In fact, Maggie imagined fangs sprouting. "Why don't you tell me just exactly what you think you're doing, luring my son into marrying you when he's all but engaged to another woman?"

Maggie simply stared at her. She wasn't easily blindsided, but the accusation had come out of nowhere. "Tucker said nothing to me about being engaged to anyone else."

"He wouldn't. Not if you were pregnant and he felt obligated to marry you."

"He told you I wasn't. Are you calling your son a liar?"

"No, I know my son. And I also know lying, scheming, manipulative women." She sat back and sipped her tea delicately.

Maggie's temper blazed but she held it back. "Meaning me."

Eileen inclined her head regally. "If the shoe fits, and all that."

Carefully, Maggie laid down her fork, determined not to give the woman the satisfaction of losing her temper. "If Tucker was engaged he'd have told me."

"He wasn't engaged. Technically. But Isabella and I have been expecting him to ask her any moment."

Isabella. He had said he'd been going out with someone, but he hadn't implied it was serious. The opposite, if anything. "Maybe you should talk to Tucker. It doesn't sound like he's on the same wavelength as the two of you." And if he had been, she was going to clean his clock for saying he'd marry her.

Eileen's expression changed to one of bewilderment. "I don't understand it. Why on earth would Tucker want to *marry* you?"

Maggie put her hands together in her lap and squeezed. *You must not slap her, no matter how much she deserves it.* "As opposed to sleep with me and dump me?" she asked sweetly.

"That's not what I said, or meant. I simply wondered why he wants to marry you."

"Ask Tucker." She stared at Eileen as her lips

tightened. "Oh, I get it. You're afraid to go after Tucker. So you thought you'd take me down and solve the problem."

"Take you down?" She looked horrified. "What a vulgar expression."

"Yeah, that's me. Just call me Officer Vulgar." Maggie got up, threw her napkin down, fished money out of her pocket and tossed it on the table. "That should cover my lunch. Just so you don't think I'm also a mooch. I suggest you talk to your son if you want the down low and dirty. You're not getting it from me." She marched out of the restaurant, head held high, holding on to her anger so she wouldn't have to admit to the hurt.

By the time she got home that afternoon, her anger, which she'd been forced to put aside while she worked, returned tenfold. What was Tucker thinking to tell her he'd marry her if he was involved with someone else? And even if that wasn't true, and she suspected it wasn't, what was he doing having a mother who was such a pain in the ass? Maggie had known Eileen didn't like her, but she hadn't honestly thought she detested her.

She pulled on her shorts, tank and boxing gloves and went to burn off some of her mad.

AS THEY'D ARRANGED, Tucker went to Maggie's after he left the office so they could work on the guest list. It still felt a little weird to think he was getting married in just a couple of days, but knowing he was helping Maggie made him feel good. Besides, it wouldn't last forever and then they could get back to their lives.

Maggie was undoubtedly right that they shouldn't have sex. I mean, how hard could it be? He'd just think of her as his buddy, as he'd done since high school. Almost one of the guys. Simple. All he had to do was forget about the way she kissed him. And his reaction when he saw her at the restaurant. And… He shook his head. From now on any thoughts of Maggie in a sexual manner were strictly forbidden.

He heard the beat of the music through the front door. Finding it unlocked, he opened it and walked in. Really old, classic rock. He wouldn't have figured her for a classic-rock kind of girl, but the Stones' "Sympathy for the Devil" blared out amazingly loud. He found her in a bedroom she'd obviously converted into her workout room. Halting on the threshold, his mouth went dry. *Oh, Mama.* She wore a skimpy tank top, short shorts and boxing gloves and was whaling on a punching bag.

She didn't look like one of the guys, that was for damn sure. She looked… Oh, man, she looked *hot*.

Hands off, he told himself. He watched her for a moment and since she obviously didn't see him, he walked over and turned the music down. She glanced at him with anything but a friendly expression in those amazing green eyes of hers.

He tucked his hands in his pockets. "Hey, Maggie."

"Hey, Tucker." She delivered a particularly nasty roundhouse kick to the bag, dropped her hands and shook out her shoulders. He glanced away, reminding himself that he didn't want to screw up their friendship.

"So, Tucker, why didn't you tell me you were *practically* engaged when you agreed to marry me?"

"Come again?" He stared at her blankly.

"Isabella. Does the name ring any bells?"

"Where did you hear about Isabella? And I wasn't engaged to her."

"All but, according to my source."

"Then your source is full of shit."

Maggie laughed and took a seat on the

weight bench. "You shouldn't talk that way about your mother."

"My mother told you I was engaged to Isabella? Why would she do that?" Especially since she knew it wasn't true.

"Give the man a cigar. Yes, your mother and I had a lovely lunch today. Remind me to do it again, sometime. Like, maybe sometime in the next century."

He took a seat beside her and pinched the bridge of his nose. "Damn, I thought she took the news awfully well. I should have known."

"Looks like. Why didn't you tell me?" She struggled with her glove and Tucker took one of her hands in his to help her take it off, then tackled the other one, ignoring how she tried to jerk her hands free of him.

"Because I was not, and have never been, engaged or almost engaged to anyone, including Isabella. Before you, that is." Okay, there was one woman, but that was a long time ago and not relevant to the discussion.

Maggie stood and paced away. "Your mother hates me. We can't get married. It was a stupid, stupid idea anyway."

"It wasn't stupid. My mother doesn't hate you, she just doesn't know you. And she has some wacko ideas about who I should marry, but it's none of her business who I do or don't decide to marry."

She turned back to him, frowning. "I don't want to cause trouble between you. Especially because of a fake marriage."

"You won't. Don't worry about it. I'll handle my mother."

"Tucker, are you sure you want to do this?"

He smiled. "Oddly enough, I am."

"Well, then at the least we shouldn't have the wedding at her house. Not considering how she feels about the whole thing. Let's just go to the JP."

"I'll talk to her," he repeated. "We're still having it at my parents' place. It will look better that way."

"Oh, yes, let's," she said. "Just what I want to do is say vows in front of a woman who hates my guts."

He walked over to her and put his hand on her shoulder. He turned her so he could scan her face and didn't like what he saw. There was temper in her eyes, but there was hurt, as well. "She hurt your feelings, didn't she? What did she say to you?"

She hunched her shoulder. "Nothing important. Just enough to let me know she isn't in favor of the marriage."

She wouldn't bad-mouth his mother, no matter how well deserved. It didn't surprise him, but it touched him. And it really burned him to know that his mother had chosen to hurt his bride, fake or not.

It took him a while but he managed to soothe Maggie's fears and joke her out of the bad mood she was in. By the time she went off to shower he figured he'd taken care of one part of the problem. His mother would have to wait until morning, but he intended to pay her a call, bright and early.

THE NEXT MORNING Tucker showed up at his parents' house so early he caught his mother in her robe. She looked happy to see him, fussing over him and asking if he'd eaten breakfast.

He sat down at the table. "Coffee's fine. I've got to get to work. I just came by to ask you what the hell you think you're doing, going behind my back to harass Maggie."

Her mouth opened and closed like a guppy's. "I did no such thing. I asked her to lunch to get better acquainted. If she's telling you lies—"

He held up a hand. "Can the innocent act,

Mom. Maggie wouldn't tell me exactly what you said, beyond some damn lie about me and Isabella, but whatever you said, it upset her."

"I told her you were all but engaged." She sniffed. "Which is true, Tucker, you know it is."

"Mom, I had a few dates with the woman. Trust me, we weren't talking marriage." She started to speak but he cut her off. "But she's not important. Maggie, and the way you treat her, is what's important here."

Her face crumpled. "Tucker, you can't really mean to marry that woman. Maggie Barnes?" she said, with just enough attitude to really piss him off.

He stood up. "I'm marrying Maggie tomorrow. We can either do it nicely and happily here or we'll do it at the justice of the peace's office. In which case you won't be invited."

"Tucker!"

"You've got a choice, Mom. You can either accept Maggie and treat her with the respect my bride deserves or you can forget about seeing me anytime in the foreseeable future."

"Tucker!" Her eyes were wide with shock. "You'd disown your own mother?"

Since he'd vented, most of his anger had passed and he looked at her in exasperation. "Of course I wouldn't disown you. You're my mother, regardless of what you say or do that I don't like. But I won't put up with you disrespecting Maggie. Not now when she's my fiancée and not later, when she's my wife. Are we clear?"

His mother stood, as well, pulling herself together. "Perfectly. Your father and I insist you have the wedding here. I'll talk to Maggie and apologize for whatever I inadvertently said to upset her."

Inadvertent, his ass. But he let it pass. He had to admire how quickly and gracefully she'd bowed to defeat. "I'd appreciate that. I'll give you the number of guests who'll attend as soon as we know."

Getting married was more complicated than he'd realized. He wondered if *being* married would be just as complex. Or would it be worse?

CHAPTER EIGHT

THE NEXT DAY, Maggie and Tucker recited their vows in the Joneses' living room. Maggie thought the whole thing had a little bit of a surreal feel to it. Almost as if it were happening to someone else.

"You may now kiss the bride," Reverend Crane said.

Tucker took Maggie in his arms and kissed her. It was brief, but it felt more real than anything else that had happened that day.

He smiled down at her and said, "You clean up good."

She laughed. "Flatterer."

"If you want the truth, you look gorgeous."

She ignored the note of sincerity in his voice. Best not go there. "All brides are beautiful. It's a requirement," Maggie said, getting her stride back. She couldn't help smiling. "But thanks."

"You're as beautiful today as I've ever seen

you," he said and took her hand as they turned to face their families and friends.

He's just being nice, she told the fluttering in her stomach. *Don't make too much of it.*

"Maggie, you look stunning," Delilah said a short time later as she hugged her. "Your gown is absolutely perfect for you."

Maggie was glad she'd listened to her mother and bought the long white gown that she'd seen at the first shop they'd entered. She'd fallen instantly in love with it. Strapless and slim-fitting, it was deceptively simple except for a little beadwork on the bodice. Though it wasn't traditional, she thought it suited her. And judging from the appreciative expression in Tucker's eyes whenever he looked at her, he more than agreed.

And she was glad she'd asked her pastor to marry them, after all. After thinking it over, she'd decided that she should. Once they'd decided against doing the deed at the justice of the peace's office, there really hadn't been a choice. First of all, her parents wouldn't have understood why she didn't ask him, and worse, the reverend himself would have been terribly hurt if Maggie, who'd grown up going to his church, didn't ask him to perform the ceremony.

If she'd thought about Vegas in time all this would be over by now. But neither she nor Tucker had. Maybe she was traditional, after all. She stifled a tiny pang, wishing that she could have been in love and getting married for real. *Focus on your goal,* she reminded herself. She shot a glance at Tucker, who was smiling at her. The side benefits weren't too bad, either, she conceded. It was going to be very interesting being married to Tucker.

"Thanks," she said to Delilah as Cameron hugged her and then claimed the right as one of her oldest friends to kiss the bride.

"You look incredible, Mrs. Jones," he said, his gray eyes twinkling. "And very happy."

"I am," she told him, realizing it was true.

"I'm really happy for you," Lana Randolph, Cam's sister-in-law, said as she hugged her. "But I'm still sad you're moving."

"I'm not moving very far. I'll still be living in Aransas City," Maggie said, returning the hug. She reflected that she was lucky to have friends like Lana and Delilah. Neither had said a word to her, although they had to suspect the real reason for the hasty marriage since they'd both seen her with Grace and, furthermore, knew she hadn't been dating Tucker. Lana, who was a doctor at the clinic in town, had even examined the baby for Maggie and pronounced her healthy. And Delilah witnessed the scene at the restaurant, so she definitely knew something was up.

But apparently, neither of her friends had given voice to their suspicions around their husbands. Gabe wouldn't have said anything, but Cam, at least, would have ragged on her about her decision to marry Tucker so suddenly if he knew the truth.

"But you won't be living next door to us. It's not the same," Lana said.

"Move over and let me kiss the bride," Gabe said, and did so as Lana talked to Tucker.

"You're a lucky man, Tucker," Gabe said a moment later.

Tucker grinned as he shook hands with Gabe. "You got that right."

Maggie wondered if he really felt lucky or he was just agreeing for form's sake. He seemed happy, laughing with their friends. He wore a navy suit with a white shirt and a beautiful silk tie, and he looked to-die-for handsome.

Later, they went outside to have a brief moment alone. "Have I mentioned how beautiful you look tonight?" Tucker asked her.

"Once or twice. Do you mean it?" Well, now she sounded pathetic. "Never mind. Forget I asked."

"I wouldn't say it if I didn't mean it. Come on, Maggie. You had to look in the mirror." He put his hand on her shoulder and rubbed it gently. "You know you look gorgeous."

She didn't know what to say to that, so she changed the subject. "Tucker, I don't want you to regret this."

"Marrying you?" He gave her a charming smile. "Maggie, the only thing I regret is that I'm not going to be taking that beautiful dress off my gorgeous bride tonight." He paused and added, "Am I?"

Maggie laughed. "You know the answer to that."

"Yeah," he said. "I was just checking to see if you'd changed your mind."

She smiled. "Nope. Why, are you having second thoughts?"

"It's hard not to when the bride in question looks like you do."

Gazing into his eyes set her stomach to fluttering. Tucker grasped both her shoulders gently and stared at her a long moment. She knew he was going to kiss her. Instead of backing away, which was the smart thing to do, she stood still and willed him to do it.

"Tucker, really," his mother said from behind them, clearly disapproving.

"Just as well," he murmured so that only Maggie heard, and kissed her briefly. He smiled at Maggie and released her. "What's wrong, Mom? Can't a man kiss his bride?"

Maggie sensed a tension between them. She hated that she was the cause of it, and she knew she was even though Tucker would deny it if she said anything.

Maggie knew nothing less than the fear of losing her son would have made Eileen Jones apologize to her for "upsetting" her as she'd done the day after their abortive lunch. She had to give the woman credit. She'd swallowed her pride and begged Maggie's forgiveness very nicely. If Maggie hadn't been a cop who dealt with good liars on a daily basis, she might have believed she meant it.

Eileen didn't respond to his question. Instead she spoke to Maggie. "Were you planning on throwing the bouquet?"

"I hadn't, but I can do it if you think I should. There aren't many single women here, though." In fact, she could only think of three, not counting

Maggie's spinster aunt, who was at least seventy-five. Oh, Lord, that would be a hoot to see. Aunt Martha would probably knock over the other women in her haste to get to the thing.

"That's entirely up to you. But if you're going to throw the bouquet and garter you'll need to do it soon. Tucker said you had to leave in an hour to catch your plane."

"Are you wearing a garter?" Tucker asked with interest.

Maggie sent him a mischievous smile. "Of course. It's my something blue."

"In that case, Mom, lead the way." He took Maggie's hand and they walked toward the living room.

"The house looks really beautiful, Mrs. Jones. I love the way you arranged the flowers," Maggie said, mindful of her resolve to get along with Tucker's mother. "Tucker and I really appreciate you letting us hold the wedding and reception here. It was so sweet of you and Mr. Jones."

Eileen smiled and for the first time Maggie didn't feel her disapproval. "Thank you, dear. We were happy to do it. And call us Harvey and Eileen, please."

It struck Maggie where she'd seen that smile before. Tucker looked like his father with the dark hair and blue eyes, while his mother was a petite blond beauty. But he'd inherited his smile from Eileen.

Just before they walked into the room Tucker released Maggie's hand and put his arm around his mother, hugging her. "Thanks, Mom."

She looked up at her son and placed a hand on his cheek. "I want you to be happy, Tucker."

"I am," he said and smiled at Maggie. "Trust me, I am."

"Then that's all that matters. I'll go gather the women for the bouquet tossing."

"Tucker, wait." Maggie put a hand on his arm to stop him from entering the room. "I don't want to cause trouble between you and your mom."

"I told you before, you won't. We're fine."

"What did you say to her, Tucker?"

"Nothing for you to worry about. I told her that you were about to become my wife and she needs to treat you with respect."

"That was sweet of you."

"Like I said, babe, anything for you. Let's go take that garter off," he said.

TUCKER HAD WANTED to stay at The Mansion in Dallas, but Maggie had vetoed it as too expensive and suggested they stay at one of the D-FW airport hotels. He gave in, even though he didn't intend for her to pay for anything involving the honeymoon. That part had been his idea and he was paying for it.

Tucker wheeled their bags in behind her and took them to the bedroom. One nice big bed. And a sofa bed in the other room, he thought regretfully.

What was wrong with him? He'd agreed to marry Maggie and live with her as a friend. He had no business thinking of sharing her bed, taking off her wedding dress… He shook his head to clear the image of peeling Maggie out of that long, slim, white dress. It's just the circumstances, he thought. Bride and groom, honeymoon, yada yada. Once they settled in to day-to-day life, he'd be able to see her as he always had. A good friend.

Who happened to be gorgeous and totally hot.

Damn. He left the bags and came out of the bedroom. Maggie had immediately kicked off her shoes and had gone to look out the window. Their room was on the side of the hotel that overlooked a garden, fortunately, instead of a parking lot.

She'd changed out of her wedding dress, much to Tucker's disappointment. She still looked great, though. She wore a short, sexy skirt and a V-necked sweater that clung to her amazing curves. Curves he needed to ignore. He'd changed into khakis and a button-down shirt, since he saw no point in taking a suit he wouldn't wear to Colorado.

He went to the minibar and popped the cork on the bottle of champagne, then poured a couple of glasses and walked over to Maggie.

"Did you arrange this?" she asked, accepting a glass.

"It seemed appropriate. It is our wedding night." He clinked his glass against hers and said, "Bottoms up."

She laughed and sipped. "Very romantic. Is that how you wow all the women?"

He smiled and took a seat. "No, but romance isn't the point of our marriage, is it? I should have said, to Grace." He raised his glass and they toasted the baby.

She sat beside him and sighed. "Are you sorry I got you into this?"

"No, I'm a big boy. I could have said no."

"Why did you agree, Tucker?"

He considered her. "Are you having cold feet again, Maggie?"

"No. Not really. But I'm wondering how you're going to deal with several months of celibacy."

He shrugged. "It's not that big a deal. I haven't had a relationship in—" He stopped and thought about it. "Seven months. About. Maybe a little longer."

"You don't have to have a relationship to have sex," she said.

"I do. At least, I do now. I like to get to know a woman before we go to bed together." Her expression was so deeply suspicious he nearly laughed. "I told you I wasn't in to meaningless sex."

"What about Isabella? You dated her several times, didn't you?"

"Yeah. But we hadn't made it to that stage."

"Why?"

"Is this how you grill your suspects?"

"I wasn't grilling you. I'm just curious about the woman your mother said you were practically engaged to."

"She's a nice woman. But she wasn't anyone I wanted to be serious about. Which I think she knew. And that's why I didn't sleep with her. My mother—well, you have to take what she says with a grain of salt."

"Yeah, a grain she'd like me to choke on."

He barely managed to swallow his champagne. "I thought you two were getting along better?"

"We are. At least, she's nice to my face. But

I know she's wishing I'd fall down an open manhole or something. Preferably before I get pregnant with any little Joneslets."

He laughed so hard he had to hold his side. "I don't think she's that bad," he finally managed to say.

"Huh." She took another sip of champagne. "So, who was the last woman you were seriously involved with and why didn't you marry her?"

"You believe in getting it right out there, don't you?"

"I think it's important that we know more about each other," she said solemnly.

"And besides, you're curious."

She dimpled and toasted him. "That, too."

Tucker's lips twitched. "My last relationship ended about seven months ago. She dumped me for a doctor, but I didn't want to marry her anyway, so it was fine by me. Now, what about you, Maggie? How are you going to deal with being celibate for months?"

She blew out a breath. "Trust me, it won't be a problem. My last relationship was six years ago. Right before I moved back to Aransas City. It didn't work out," she said briefly.

Apparently that's all she meant to say on the subject. He tucked that information away to talk about later, but zeroed in on one aspect he found hard to believe. "You haven't had sex in six years?"

She sipped her champagne, then set the glass down. "Six and a half."

"Good God," he said blankly. "That's a long time." Especially for someone as passionate as he suspected Maggie was.

She shrugged. "I'm not very good at picking the right man. So after the last one, I decided I wasn't going to sleep with anyone again until I was damn sure it wouldn't be a mistake."

"He must have hurt you a lot. I'm sorry."

"Do you mind if we don't talk about it? It's not my favorite topic of conversation."

He got up to pour them more champagne. "Okay by me. What do you want to do, then?"

"We've got champagne and a long night ahead of us. I know just the thing."

Somehow he doubted that what popped into his head was the same thing Maggie had in mind.

CHAPTER NINE

"GET YOUR MIND out of the gutter, Jones."

He laughed, finished pouring and brought her glass to her. "I didn't say a word." He sat again.

"Trust me, your expression said it all." Not that she held it against him. Given her job, she spent the majority of her time around men. She understood very well the way their minds worked.

"What do you have in mind?"

"Movies. Old movies and champagne. How does that sound?"

He grimaced. "Okay. Only we swear we'll never tell anyone that we watched movies on our wedding night."

"It's a deal." She flicked on the TV and started channel surfing. "There doesn't seem to be much on."

"Why am I not surprised?" He took off his shoes and socks and stretched out his legs, propping them on the coffee table. "We could watch old episodes of *NYPD Blue.*"

"Let's not and say we did." She continued flipping until she got to a repeat of *L.A. Law.* "How's this?"

Tucker gave her a thumbs-down.

"There's not even a decent movie," she said. "Here, you do it and I'll get us more champagne." She went to the bar and poured them both some more. "At this rate we're going to run out before we even find a movie to watch." She put the bottle back in the cooler, sat down and took a sip. "What's that? It's got Susan Hayward in it. My dad used to say I had hair the color of hers."

Tucker looked at her. "Yours is prettier."

She narrowed her eyes at him. "What are you after, Tucker?"

"Nothing." He raised a hand and said solemnly, "I speak the truth."

She punched him in the arm. "Ha. Do you know what movie this is?"

"Yeah. I saw it once when I was home with the flu. *Back Street* is the name of it. It's about a woman and her doomed love affair with a married man."

Her stomach pitched. Even after all this time, it still bothered her. "Can you change it?"

"Sure." He switched to another channel that

was showing an Arnold Schwarzenegger movie. "How's this?"

"Fine." They watched Arnold blow up a compound in search of his daughter. Maggie wondered what it said about her that she'd rather watch an action movie than a romance.

"Maggie? Don't you like romances?"

"Not doomed ones. Besides, I don't think love affairs with married men are very romantic."

He took a sip of his drink and studied her. "Sounds like there's a story there," he said, echoing what she'd said to him a few days before.

She didn't answer immediately. He didn't say anything. He wouldn't push her to share, she knew. But maybe it was time she talked about it. She never had, not once in all these years. She'd nearly told Lana one time, but the moment had passed and she hadn't. Maybe she shouldn't tell Tucker, either. It didn't exactly cast her in a good light.

"I was twenty-one," she said. "When I lost my virginity."

The segue didn't appear to bother him. "You waited longer than a lot of people do."

"Yeah, I did. I wanted it to be special."

"Something tells me it wasn't a great experience for you."

"Oh, the sex was good. He was very… skilled." And she'd been like a ripe plum just waiting to be picked. "I was fresh out of the academy and so naive I probably had a sign tattooed on my forehead that said, 'This girl's from Podunk and dumb as a post.'"

He frowned at her. "Aren't you being a little hard on yourself?"

Maggie shrugged. "No. You haven't heard the whole story yet. He was about ten years older than me. Smooth and very charming. Good-looking. And married."

"Ah. That explains your aversion to the movie. Did you know?"

He didn't appear judgmental, which made her feel a little better. "Not at first. Later I did. But—"

"Let me guess," Tucker interrupted. "He told you he was getting divorced."

Maggie nodded. "I told you I was naive. He said he was legally separated and he wasn't living with her and the divorce should be final, oh, anytime now." It still amazed her she could have been so gullible.

"It was a lie. Damn, Maggie, that's terrible."

"Yeah." She sipped her drink reflectively before continuing. "Two months after I first slept with him, his wife found out about us and called me. Seems she was six weeks pregnant and wanted her husband to stop fooling around with the slutty cop."

Tucker said something violent and obscene regarding what he'd like to do to the man. It perfectly described how she felt about the matter. To her surprise, she laughed.

"Well, I didn't do that, although I'd have loved to. But when he tried to convince me he'd only slept with her once and it really didn't have to ruin the beautiful thing we had together I wanted to throw up."

"What did you do to him, Maggie?"

Remembering, she smiled. "I threw him out of my apartment and locked the door. Then I flushed his keys down the toilet."

Tucker looked disappointed. "That's not nearly bad enough for what he did to you."

"It gets better. He had to walk home. It was ten miles. In Dallas, at night."

"Why didn't he just call a cab?"

She bit her lip, finding humor in the situation for the first time. "No money. I picked his pocket. And this was in the days before everyone had a cell phone. He broke into his car, I guess he was going to try to hot-wire it.

But I called my station house and anonymously reported a car theft in progress when I heard the car alarm go off. Even though he got off eventually, he was hauled in and charged with attempted grand theft auto. No ID, no money. Very suspicious guy breaking into a BMW." She laughed. "That was much better than him just having to walk home."

Tucker smiled but then sobered. He reached for her hand and held it, squeezing gently. "I hate that he hurt you like he did. Damn it, he should be strung up. Your first relationship should have been good for you."

She shrugged, still angry at herself over the whole thing. "I hate that I was so stupid."

"You weren't stupid. You were naive and young and he took advantage of you."

She looked at him and shook her head, pulling her hand out of his. "Tucker, I had an affair with a married man. It was wrong and I knew it. Believing he was getting divorced makes it only marginally better."

"You're too hard on yourself," he insisted.

"Have you ever been with a married woman?"

He looked chagrined. "Yes."

Maggie said shrewdly, "You didn't know she was married, did you?"

"No, but that's beside the point. Even if I'd known I'd still have done it."

Maggie wasn't so sure of that. "You're just saying that to make me feel better."

"You're not the only one who's ever been gullible." He reached for his drink.

"Tucker, the last word I'd use to describe you is *gullible*. Just because you didn't know she was married—"

"No, not her."

He was silent for a long moment, so she said, "You don't have to tell me."

He shrugged. "I'd been working in San Antonio for a few years. She was a lawyer with the same firm. Blond, beautiful. Ambitious. We started dating. I fell hard for her. So hard I even started thinking marriage." He laughed, not happily. "Fortunately, before I did anything completely stupid, such as ask her to marry me, I overheard a phone conversation she had with a friend of hers. Seems I wasn't the only man she was dating. She was juggling two of us. He was a wealthy banker. She was trying to decide who had the most money and was talking about hiring a private detective. She wanted to know who to dump and who to con into marriage."

Maggie stared at him. "You're kidding."

"Nope. She said I was better-looking but she suspected he had more money and she had to be practical."

"God, that's cold."

"Yeah, tell me about it. I was a little cynical for a while, but I got over it. The experience didn't do my ego much good, though."

He acted as if it hadn't affected him, but she thought it had more than he'd admitted. "You don't hate women." Who could have blamed him if he had?

"No, I like women. I'm just very careful about who I get involved with now."

"I imagine you would be," Maggie said. "But, Tucker, she was the stupid one, not you."

"I was supposed to be out of the office that day. If she'd known I was anywhere near I'm sure she wouldn't have been talking so freely."

Maggie shook her head. "Not because of that. She was stupid not to realize there's a hell of a lot more to you than good looks and the bucks."

He stared at her a long moment, then smiled slowly. "Maggie, that's the nicest thing you've ever said to me."

She started to deny it but he was probably right. "Tucker, can I ask you something?"

"Sure."

"I asked you before but you didn't really answer. Why did you agree to marry me?"

"A number of reasons. But the main one is I care about you. I want you to be happy. Grace makes you happy. I wanted you to have a chance to keep her."

She wasn't sure that was the entire reason, but she didn't think he'd admit to anything else, so she let it pass. "We might find her mother. There's still a chance. And there's still a chance CPS won't let us have her, after all." Thinking about that depressed her. She could apply to foster another child, even without Tucker, but she didn't want another baby. She wanted Grace. "I guess the marriage would be even more temporary than we thought if that happens." That scenario also depressed her for reasons she didn't care to examine closely.

He moved nearer to her, then put his arm around her and hugged her companionably. "Don't borrow trouble. And another thing, I think we should stop referring to this marriage as temporary. It serves no purpose, and if we want people to believe our marriage is authentic, then we need to treat it like it is."

She leaned her head against his shoulder. "Is this a way of convincing me I should rethink my ban on sex?"

Tucker chuckled. "No." He was quiet a moment, his hand rubbing gently up and down her arm. "Why, are you rethinking it?"

She turned to look up at him. He wasn't smiling now, and he looked at her with a hunger she hadn't expected. She moved away quickly, before she did something stupid. Like kiss him. And she knew exactly where that would lead them. "Are you?"

His gaze zeroed in on her mouth. "If I said no, you'd know I was lying. I was the one who suggested we make it real in the first place. So, yeah, I've thought about it. But…I think you're right. It could screw up our friendship. And that's important to me. More important than a roll in the sheets."

"You looked at me like you wanted to…" Not wanting to say the words, she let her voice trail away. Damn it, she should never have started this conversation. What did it matter why he'd married her? He'd agreed, they were married, and that was that.

"Just because I might think about it now and then doesn't mean I'm going to do anything."

"Because going to bed together would be a mistake."

"Right."

"Right," she said, annoyed though she knew she had no right to be. "So, that's that. Why are we talking about it?"

"Because you asked me if—"

"Stop." She held up her hand, laughing. "I should know better than to ask a lawyer a rhetorical question. I've got an idea. You go pour us more champagne. I'm going to put my jammies on. And no, I'm not wearing what my mother packed for me to wear."

"Filmy nightgown?" he asked with a leer.

"Of course. But you'll just have to make do with the real me." Boxers and a T-shirt were infinitely safer. And she needed safe. Because Tucker Jones was very, very dangerous. To her peace of mind, at the very least.

And what about your heart?

She couldn't afford to fall in love with Tucker. She'd fallen for the wrong man before. Had her heart broken before. She'd been with three men and every single one had been the wrong man for her. She damn near hadn't recovered from the last one. Six and a half years ago, the breakup that had sent her running home, heart-

sick and convinced she'd never fall in love
again. Dead certain she didn't *want* to ever fall
in love again.

She was not going to fall in love with Tucker.
That could only lead to disaster. A disaster she
couldn't afford.

CHAPTER TEN

IT DIDN'T SURPRISE Tucker that Maggie took to skiing like a natural. Although he knew how to ski, he wasn't too sure about his teaching capabilities, so he thought she'd be better off with a ski instructor, at least initially. Their first full day in Steamboat, Maggie took a lesson in the morning and then Tucker skied with her that afternoon. He liked sharing one of his favorite sports with her. He didn't even mind when she crashed into him and they both fell.

He liked watching her concentrate, liked seeing her deliberate movements as she focused on what she was doing. She was a natural athlete, not to mention extremely competitive. He couldn't help laughing at her frustration over not becoming a world-class skier instantly.

"Maggie, there's a learning curve in skiing, just like in everything else."

"I don't like the bunny slope," she grumbled.

"Why can't I ski things like that?" She pointed to a run that was at least a single black diamond if not a double diamond. Expert. Steep, bumpy. He shuddered, thinking of a novice skier on one of those babies.

"Down, killer. Maybe next trip. Besides, you went down a run from the top. Most people don't do that their first day out."

"It was an easy one, you said so yourself."

He laughed at her pouting and didn't manage to get her to quit until the lifts closed. "Can you spell overachiever?" he asked her as they entered their condo.

"I'm not an overachiever," she said automatically, peeling out of her jacket and hanging it on the rack by the door. She linked her hands behind her back, stretched and groaned. "I have a feeling I'm going to be sore."

The way she did that thrust her breasts into prominent relief, something he didn't think she realized. But man, oh, man, he noticed. He shook his head. *Get a grip.*

"That's what hot tubs are for," he managed to say.

They had reservations that evening at one of Tucker's favorite restaurants, Café Diva. They soaked in the hot tub—another experience that brought him both pain and pleasure. Maggie in a bathing suit was something to see. It didn't matter how much he lectured himself about looking at her as a friend, he still had eyes, didn't he?

After they cleaned up, Tucker watched Maggie flip through a sheaf of papers and mutter. His stomach growled and he wondered if Maggie would ever put away the paperwork about foster care that she'd been absorbed in for the last half hour. She'd pulled it out the day before and had been reading questions to him that they would have to answer in an interview. It seemed invasive as hell to him, but Maggie had warned him that it would be.

"We're going to be late to dinner," he said as his stomach growled again. She had to be hungry, didn't she? They'd both had water and munched on trail mix for lunch and hadn't eaten anything else.

Maggie glanced up at him and frowned. "Why do they want to know about our past relationships? I can see why they want to know about the current one, but my past is none of their business."

Maggie had been freaking out about the list of questions ever since she'd first looked at it. She said she'd only glanced at it before and this was the first time that she'd gone through all the actual questions the caseworker would be likely to ask.

"You don't have to tell them the whole truth, you know. Be vague."

"The whole truth? We're already going to have to lie like convicts about when and how and why we decided to marry, and about why we want to be foster parents and when we knew we wanted to do that. Now—" she waved a sheet of paper "—this is just more stuff to have to lie about."

"Why are you so worried? We'll work it out."

She ignored him. "I'm not telling them anything about him," she said. "I'm just going to act as if that whole…revolting episode never happened."

Tucker assumed she was referring to being with the married slime. "It happened a long time ago," he agreed. "That shouldn't have a bearing on your parenting abilities."

"Right. I was young, stupid and it has nothing to do with me now." She looked down and scribbled something on a piece of paper. "And I'm not talking about Spencer, either."

"Maggie?"

"Hmm." She wasn't looking at him, but frowned at the papers in front of her.

"Who's Spencer?"

She looked up and met his gaze. Her eyes narrowed suspiciously. "How do you know about him?"

"Because you just mentioned his name. Who is he? Not the man—"

"No. Not him."

He waited but she didn't seem to want to add to that. "Is this another story I need to know about?" he said when she didn't speak.

"No. I don't want to talk about it."

Ho-kay. Touchy subject, obviously. "Then why did you bring it up?"

"Because I wasn't thinking." She got to her feet. "Let's go eat. I'm starving."

He followed her lead, but he had to wonder about the other man she wasn't talking about. Should he push her to talk, or should he just let her be? Because there was definitely a story here.

Before long they were being shown into the Café Diva. A small, elegant restaurant with a gorgeous mahogany bar and a wood-burning fireplace, it had a cozy, romantic ambience. The snow falling outside completed the perfect picture. The walls were graced with paintings from local artists and it was also known for its wonderful food and an excellent wine list.

Tucker greeted the owner and their waitress by name, as he'd known both of them for several years. He introduced Maggie as his wife and they were suitably surprised and pleased to have the honeymooning couple eat with them.

"Do you know everyone in this restaurant?" Maggie asked him after the waitress left to get their drinks.

"Not everyone. But I've been coming to Steamboat for years now and always make sure to eat here at least once. It's one of my favorite places." He watched her reach behind her back and frown.

"What's wrong?"

"Nothing. I wish I hadn't left my Glock at home. I feel naked without it."

Tucker laughed. "Believe me, I'd have noticed if you were. I thought you said since you were going out of state it would be easier not to carry it." He realized she'd taken her customary position at the table, with her back to a wall and where she could see the door. He wondered if all cops did that and, if so, what did they do when a bunch of them got together?

Maggie shrugged. "It's still weird."

Tucker patted her hand. "Steamboat's pretty tame. I doubt you'll need it. There's a little crime around the mountain during high season, with all the transients and tourists, but not much. It's a lot like Aransas City in a way. In town the residents don't even lock their doors."

"It does seem like a nice town. When did you start coming here?"

"My parents used to come years ago when I was a kid and they'd bring me."

The waitress served their wine and brought them some crusty French bread and olive oil with balsamic vinegar. Maggie ate a bite and said, "Oh, this is delicious."

They talked a bit until the waitress came back and discussed the menu with them. After they ordered, Maggie said, "Why did you decide to move back to the Aransas Bay area? I heard you were doing well in San Antonio. Didn't you like it?"

"I liked it. I just decided I didn't want to spend the rest of my life there. I missed the coast, for one thing."

"I know what you mean. I missed it, too, when I lived in Dallas. I didn't expect to, but I did."

Before long their entrées arrived and they both began to eat. "Why did you move to Dallas?" Tucker asked Maggie. "Was it just to go to the police academy?"

She nodded. "That was part of it. Plus, I

wanted to get out of Aransas City. I wanted out of the hick town and into the big city. I was all set to accomplish great things. That didn't exactly happen." She laughed and Tucker detected a note of bitterness.

"Did you like being on the Dallas police force?"

"Mostly. Some of it was hard. Some of the crime scenes we went to were…pretty brutal," she admitted. "But most of the time I liked my job."

"So you didn't leave Dallas to get away from police work."

She put down her fork and looked at him. "I came back to Aransas City because I wanted to. Why don't we just leave it at that?"

Clearly, something had happened while she was in Dallas that she wasn't ready to talk about. He suspected it had something to do with the man she'd mentioned, Spencer. He wanted to ask her about him, but he figured she'd tell him when she was good and ready. He'd already discovered that Maggie could be very stubborn and closemouthed, so he let the subject drop.

"Whatever you say. Did you want to get some dessert? They have a dynamite crème brûlée."

Maggie sent him a grateful glance. "How

about we split it? I don't want to eat a whole one. I'm already stuffed from eating the entrée."

They ordered the dessert and talked about skiing and their plans for the next day. While they were eating dessert, Maggie said, "Weren't you a partner in a big firm in San Antonio? Wasn't that hard to walk away from?"

Unlike Maggie, that wasn't one of the things that bothered him to talk about. He'd already told her the only thing about his past that still stuck in his craw. Admitting that he'd let Leila Anderson play him had been difficult. In fact, he was a little surprised he'd told Maggie about her.

Maggie took another bite of dessert. "You don't have to answer if you don't want."

He shook his head. "No, I don't mind. I got tired of the pressure, and the pace. You know the difference between a small town like Aransas City and a big city. I discovered I was tired of that more frenetic lifestyle, so I came back to the coast. I didn't want to live too close to my parents, which is why I chose Aransas City. There wasn't one instance that triggered the decision to move, but more of a gradual buildup of dissatisfaction."

"Do you think you'll stay in Aransas City?"

He smiled at her. "For the foreseeable future, anyway."

Her eyes darkened to a deep, mossy green. "I really appreciate what you're doing for me, Tucker."

"Believe me, Maggie, it hasn't been a hardship." Except one thing was becoming a hardship. Keeping his hands to himself. *It's just the honeymoon,* he told himself. *The romance of it. Once you get back home things will return to normal. Won't they?*

"That's what you say now, but that could change."

"I don't see why it should."

"You could meet another woman and…well, you'd be stuck because you're married to me. At least until we find out about Grace." She wasn't looking at him but had applied herself to the last of the dessert.

What was this about? "I'm not interested in another woman. Have I given you any reason to believe I am?"

She shot him a glance he couldn't read. "No, so don't get your shorts in a twist. But we both know the reasons behind our marriage. All I'm saying is you could have a change of heart and regret tying yourself down. Then what would we do?"

He stared at her a moment, trying to figure out

where she was coming from. It dawned on him that this might have something to do with the mysterious Spencer. "Is that what he did? Have a change of heart?"

Her eyes had changed color, they were flat and very nearly gray, with no green to be seen. "No. His heart never changed. That was the problem."

The waitress came just then to ask if they needed anything else and to give him the bill. But Tucker wasn't sure Maggie would have said any more even if they hadn't been interrupted. It appeared that this story was one he would have to drag out of Maggie in bits and pieces. If indeed he managed to get the whole story out of her at all.

CHAPTER ELEVEN

ONCE THEY RETURNED from their honeymoon and moved Maggie's belongings into Tucker's house, Maggie and Tucker became serious about becoming licensed in foster care. The preliminary training course wasn't a problem and they both soon completed it. As far as she could tell, the individual interviews that had been conducted at the CPS office had gone well. But the in-home joint interview loomed ahead of them and though Maggie wouldn't admit it to Tucker, she worried about it. And one of the major sources of her worry was that while they weren't sharing a bedroom, they had to make it look as if they were.

Of course, it had been her idea not to have sex, which she still believed was the right thing to do. And he'd agreed with her after he'd thought it over. But who knew it would be so difficult to live with a man platonically? she thought one morning.

He came into the kitchen just then, smiling that sleepy smile as he poured a cup of the coffee he couldn't function without. How was she supposed to ignore that every day? Bare-chested, wearing a pair of faded Levi's, his beard a sexy stubble on his cheeks, he made her...want.

Maybe she should just do it, she thought. She could talk Tucker into it, she was sure. They could do it, get it over with and then go on about their business.

She shook her head, marveling at how easy it was to rationalize. No, those were hormones talking. She ought to just go take a cold shower.

He sat and shook out the paper to read it, still not having spoken. She knew by now he didn't usually talk much in the morning, but how could he be so calm when today was their joint interview?

"Are you going in to work?" she asked him.

He glanced up. "Yes, why?"

"Today's the in-home joint interview," she reminded him.

He smiled. "I know. You've told me half a dozen times since yesterday. It's not until one. Plenty of time for me to get something done this morning."

"We have to do something to your bedroom. To make it look more like we share it. And the master bath, too. No woman in her right mind would give up that dream of a bathroom."

He looked really amused now, which irritated her. "I told you to take my bedroom."

"No, that wouldn't be right," she said decisively, if a bit wistfully. "I'll have to move some of my stuff in there. I should probably leave it, too, since they might visit unexpectedly. Probably will, if I had to guess."

"There's another option," Tucker said, waiting until she glanced at him to speak. "You could move into the bedroom with me."

"Oh, sure. I'm going to share a bedroom with you and not have sex with you. That's going to happen. It's hard enough to—" She broke off, annoyed at what she'd almost let slip. Tucker didn't seem to have any problems resisting her. His seeming lack of interest burned her, considering she was the one who had originally wanted to keep the marriage platonic.

He grinned. "Just a thought, babe."

A thought she was not going to explore. "Let me know when you're finished dressing and I'll start moving stuff in there. In the meantime, I'll clean up my bedroom. Don't you think it will be okay if I just shove everything into drawers and closets?"

"Beats me. I've never been interviewed for something like this. You've said they're pretty invasive."

"Invasive is one thing. Looking into a person's closets and drawers is just…sick," she decided.

Tucker laughed, reaching across the table to squeeze her hand. "Relax, Maggie. Everything's going to work out, I promise."

"I hope so."

"It will." He gave her hand a last squeeze and got up. "I'm going to shower. Maybe you ought to do yoga. Or go whale on the punching bag."

Not a bad idea, she thought. "Tucker?" He stopped at the door and glanced back at her. "Thanks."

He simply smiled and left the room. She watched him go, thinking that he looked nearly as good going as he did coming. Maggie turned her thoughts away from the tempting possibilities Tucker had brought to mind and back to the task of convincing the caseworker that she and Tucker were the perfect couple to foster a child.

THE INTERVIEW went better than Maggie had expected, and as far as she could tell, the caseworker had no problems with them. Tucker charmed her, spinning what, to Maggie, sounded like a believable story about why they wanted to be foster parents.

The woman had indeed peeked into all the rooms, but Maggie had worked hard on the master bedroom to make sure it looked lived-in by both of them. She'd even spritzed a little perfume in the master bath. She smiled, remembering Tucker's expression when he'd gone in there. He clearly hadn't expected that. Then Maggie had to show the woman where she planned to keep her weapon and assure her that it would either be locked up or on Maggie's person whenever she was at home, but she'd expected that.

The only thing Maggie hadn't anticipated, and she should have, she realized, was that the caseworker wanted to know how much interaction their extended family would have with them and the foster child, as well as their degree of acceptance. And she wanted to meet with both sets of their parents, though she said that wasn't urgent.

Maggie decided to talk to her parents that afternoon, but Tucker had wanted her with him when he told his parents about their plans. They had made arrangements to meet his folks for dinner, at a restaurant in Rockport.

She didn't expect to have a problem with her parents. They might wonder why she and Tucker wanted to be foster parents, but they certainly wouldn't throw a wrench into the works. Her mother in particular spent a lot more time worrying about her younger sister than she did Maggie.

Late that afternoon, she went into her parents' house through the back door, which was unlocked, as usual. "Mom, Dad, where are you?"

Her mother came into the kitchen, her eyes sparkling. "I'm glad you stopped by. We have some exciting news to tell you."

"Where's Dad?" She wondered what kind of news would make her normally placid mother so excited.

"He's on the phone. No, here he is now," she said as Frank walked in the room. "Tell her, Grandpa."

"Hey, Maggie," he said, though he seemed preoccupied. He turned to his wife. "Colleen, we have a meeting with the Realtor at four-thirty, so we can't talk long."

"Realtor?" Maggie echoed. "Why are you meeting a Realtor? Are you buying a new house?" She couldn't imagine it. Her parents had lived in the same small brick house for longer than Maggie had been alive.

"We're putting the house on the market. Your father's finally agreed to move."

Maggie's heart sank. She'd known her parents had been considering moving to Florida to be with her sister and her family, but she'd hoped they'd decide against it.

"Why did you decide to move so suddenly? I thought you didn't want to leave here, Dad?"

Frank grunted and took a seat at the kitchen table. "Well, Lorna's pregnant again and she wants your mother there to help her."

Pregnant? Again? "Summer's only six months old. You mean to tell me Lorna's having another baby already?" This one would make number four. Just how many children did Lorna intend to have?

"That's right. Isn't it wonderful?" her mother asked.

No, Maggie wanted to say, but she bit her tongue. "But you don't even know how long they're going to be in Florida. What if John gets transferred again?"

"Then we'll move to wherever they go." Colleen put her hand on Maggie's arm. "What's wrong, honey? Are you worried we won't see you? We can still get together at holidays and such. I know it's a big change, but Lorna needs us. With all those children…" Her voice trailed off, and she searched Maggie's face with a look of concern.

Maggie simply looked at her. She knew her parents loved her. But all her life it seemed she'd come in second to her baby sister. She didn't think her parents did it on purpose, or even realized they were playing favorites. But the fact remained, Maggie had felt like an afterthought in their lives for a long time. She moved away to stare out the window.

"Maggie, you understand, don't you? Lorna needs us."

She turned back to her mother. "Sure, Mom. I understand." She understood perfectly. Her parents might love her, but they loved her sister more. Why should it hurt? She was used to it, wasn't she?

"I was so excited I forgot you'd said you had something to tell us. What did you want to talk to us about, Maggie?"

"It doesn't matter," Maggie said. "I'll talk to you later. I've got to get back to work."

She didn't, but she couldn't stay in the house

with them and pretend everything was hunky-dory when she was embarrassingly close to tears. What difference did it make what her parents thought about her becoming a foster parent when they wouldn't even be around? She'd simply tell the caseworker that her parents didn't give a tinker's damn about her, and were moving to freaking Florida, besides. So there was no need to worry about their reaction to any foster children Maggie might or might not have.

I'm thirty-four years old, she thought. *I've been grown and on my own for a long time now. The fact that my parents are moving shouldn't be a big deal.*

But it was.

TUCKER HAD LEFT WORK early so he could talk to Maggie about the best way to approach his parents when they told them about becoming foster parents. He wanted to be prepared because he had a feeling they were going to ask some difficult questions. Particularly his father, who Tucker knew was still suspicious of their motives for getting married. When he arrived at home, he only had to follow the music to find Maggie. He tracked her down to the room they'd converted into a home gym, with a weight bench, free weights and—since Maggie had moved in—a punching bag.

Extremely loud headbanger rock and roll blared from the stereo system he'd installed. Evidently Maggie had been doing some serious boxing. She wore a tank top, shorts and her boxing gloves and was barefoot and slick with sweat. His mouth started watering and he reminded himself they had things to talk about and seducing Maggie was not on the list of smart things to do. Damn it.

He watched her for a moment, a frown gathering as he realized how savagely she was going after the bag. He'd seen her at this before, but he'd never felt raw fury coming off her in waves. Even when she'd been mad at him over his supposed engagement, she hadn't been this angry. What in the hell had happened? He hoped it wasn't something to do with Grace. Maggie clearly had no idea he was there, so he walked over and turned down the music.

"Turn it back on," she snapped. She punched the bag with her right hand. *Smack.* Then her left, a quick double jab before returning to beat the bag with her left again.

He didn't do what she'd said, just watched

her trying to decimate the bag. She apparently got tired of boxing and started with some Tae Kwon Do moves, a series of kicks interspersed with those repeated jabs.

"What's wrong?"

Smack. "Nothing's wrong." Another jab and a kick. "Turn the damn music back on."

"If nothing's wrong why are you beating the crap out of an inanimate object?"

"Because I like to." She kept at it, grunting with the effort.

"Did you talk to your parents?"

"Yes." She bit the word out as she sent a particularly hard punch into the bag. "But not about the foster parenting. They're moving, so there's no need to worry about them."

"Your parents are moving?" That was the first he'd heard of it. "Where? Why?"

She whirled and delivered a roundhouse kick to the bag. "To Florida." She hit the bag with a combination one-two jab and kick. "To be with my precious sister—" she hit the bag twice "—and their precious grandchildren."

Her breath was coming hard and her words were jerky, but he heard her clearly. He walked over to her and put his hand on her arm. "Do you want to talk about this?"

"No, I want to beat the hell out of this punching bag." She shook him off and glared at him. "Don't mess with me, Tucker. I'm not in a good mood."

He wanted to gather her in his arms and comfort her, but she was obviously not in any mood to be consoled. "Come sit down," he said and took her arm.

She resisted at first but then she let him lead her to the weight bench and sit beside her. He took one of her hands and started to pull off her glove. "You're going to hurt your hands, if you haven't already."

Her eyes were stormy. A hard, brilliant green, but Tucker saw the hurt behind the anger. Again, he wished she'd let him comfort her. It surprised him how badly he wanted to console her. "Was this move a surprise? Or had you known about it? You haven't said anything."

She shrugged and let him take off the other glove and gently massage her hands. "It wasn't a total shock. They'd been talking about it, but I didn't think they were going to go. My mother wanted to do it but my dad had been resisting."

"Why did they decide to go now?"

Her eyes were bleak, not hot with anger. Gray and empty. "Because my sister—my younger sister—is pregnant again. With her fourth child. My mother's all in to the grandma thing."

A wealth of unspoken emotion lay behind those words. He didn't need a psychology degree to understand that. "Have you told your parents how you feel about them leaving Aransas City? About them leaving you?"

"No." Wearily, she lifted a shoulder. "What's the point? They want to be with Lorna. Lorna needs them, they said. Period. End of discussion."

"You might let them know you need them, too." He looked at her hands and imagined kissing them. Then imagined going right on up her arm. To her mouth. And— *Down, boy. What the hell are you thinking?*

"I don't need them." She jerked her hands out of his. "I'm thirty-four years old, Tucker. I don't have to have my mommy and daddy live in the same town to survive."

"It's not a matter of survival." He studied her a moment, not buying the supertough act she was putting on. "Maggie, there's nothing wrong with not wanting your parents to move. I wouldn't want mine to move away. And there's nothing wrong with wanting your parents' emotional support, no matter how old you are."

"Emotional support." She gave a short, bitter

laugh and glanced away. Her voice was tight when she said, "That's a joke. It's always been Lorna. I love my sister, but…she's always been the needy one. I'm the self-sufficient one, the one who always knows what she's doing. At least, that's how they see me. And none of them, not my parents and sure as hell not my sister, even notice that occasionally I need someone, too."

"And you need someone now."

She nodded. "Yes. It's just like before. It never changes. When I moved back here from Dallas…my mother was so caught up with Lorna and her second pregnancy, I might as well not have existed."

It hurt him to hear the pain in her voice. "You needed your mother then."

She looked forlorn, something he'd never associated with Maggie before.

"Yes. I wanted someone to talk to. Someone who loved me, who cared about what happened to me. I…wasn't doing very well."

Again, he wondered what had driven her to leave Dallas. For Maggie to admit to anyone that she wasn't doing well was the same as another person telling the world they'd had a complete breakdown. "Did you find anyone else to talk to? A girlfriend, maybe?"

"No." Her gaze hardened before she rolled her shoulder and looked away. "There wasn't anyone. So I did what I always do. I sucked it up and moved on. I got over it. Talking is way overrated."

"Maggie?" He waited until she looked at him. "I know it's a long time after the fact, but you could talk to me."

Her expression softened. "Tucker, you're sweet, but I'm over that now." She blew out a breath. "I'm just overreacting to my parents moving, that's all. I'll be okay. It was just a surprise that they're actually going ahead with it."

She wasn't over it and he didn't think she'd be okay. But she didn't seem to want his help. He couldn't have said why that realization bothered him so much.

"If you ever do want to talk, come to me. Okay?"

"Okay." She put her hand on his cheek and smiled at him. "Thanks, Tucker. You're sweet," she repeated.

Sweet. His thoughts weren't so sweet. She was braless and the thin tank fit her like a second skin. He wanted to cup her breasts, take his thumbs over the peaks, strip her shirt off and see how beautiful they would be bare. Wanted to taste her, caress her, make love to her….

He raised his gaze to hers. Her breath came faster and she stared at him with parted lips, her eyes big and dark with emotion. "Tucker...I—I can't."

"Can't? Or won't?"

"It doesn't matter, does it?" She got up and walked to the door. "Sometimes I really wish I could just do what I want and not worry about the consequences. But I'm not built that way."

She left the room and Tucker blew out a breath. She was right. If they made love it would change everything between them. And he didn't want to change it, to risk... Damn it, he was falling for her.

CHAPTER TWELVE

TUCKER THOUGHT Maggie was going to lose it waiting for CPS to make up their minds over the next couple of weeks. She was grouchy, touchy and despondent. Everything that was hard to live with. Even so, he was having a devil of a time keeping his hands to himself. He wasn't sure what that said about him, that he could find a woman so attractive in such trying circumstances.

Proximity. Maybe that's all it was. He wasn't falling for her. Not really. He was living with her, for Pete's sake. Seeing her in various states of undress. Looking but never touching. It was enough to drive a man crazy.

One day Tucker got a phone call just as he was about to leave the office.

"It's your wife," his secretary told him, handing him the phone.

He took the cordless phone and walked back to his office. "Hey, Maggie. What's up?"

He hoped it was good news. The wait was wearing on them both. He'd thought his mother and father had taken the news in stride when they first told them. At least, they hadn't said much that evening. But since then, every time he talked to his mother, she asked why Tucker and Maggie weren't starting a family of their own if they wanted children. And though he hadn't told Maggie, Tucker had the feeling that his father, at the least, suspected the truth.

"Tucker, it's—wait a minute."

He heard her say something to someone else and a short while later she came back on the line.

"I can't believe it."

"Where are you? You sound like you're at the bottom of a well."

"I'm in the bathroom at the station. I was afraid I'd cry and the guys would never let me hear the end of it if they saw me leaking tears."

"What's wrong? Have they found Grace's mother?" Tucker was growing more and more worried about Maggie's reaction if and when they found the woman. Since marrying Maggie, he'd done a little research. Enough to know that in child custody cases, especially those involving foster care, judges usually came down in the birth mother's favor, especially if there was no history of abuse.

He'd brought up the possibility of the mother being found or showing up and wanting Grace back a couple of times, but Maggie wouldn't talk much about it. She simply said she'd deal with the matter when it happened. It was how she planned to deal with it that worried Tucker.

"No, we haven't found her yet. Nothing's wrong." She paused, then burst out with, "Nina called. We get to have Grace."

"Maggie, that's great." He needed to bury his reservations and his worries. This was what Maggie had wanted all along. He had to be happy for her.

"I know. I can't believe it's finally happening. Can you meet me at the house? We can pick her up anytime, they said. I think it would be best if you went, too, don't you? They'll be expecting both of us, I imagine."

"I wouldn't miss it. See you soon."

Not long afterward, Tucker walked into the house calling for Maggie. She came out of the nursery holding the car seat, but when she saw him she dropped it and launched herself into his arms, laughing. "Can you believe it? I don't think I've ever been so excited in my life."

He spun her around and started to say something but she gave him a smacking kiss on the mouth, then smiled at him. So he kissed her back. Really kissed her, as he'd been wanting to do for weeks now. He crushed her in his arms, pushed his tongue inside her mouth, and she gave a low moan, her arms tightening around his neck.

He sank into her soft mouth, tasting, lingering, then slipped his hands over her curves and caressed her. Slowly, he became aware she'd wedged one arm between them and was pushing him away. He drew back and stared down at her. Her lips were wet from his kiss and he wanted nothing more than to drown himself in her and not come up until he was finally sated.

Then he looked into her eyes and knew it wasn't going to happen.

"Tucker—"

He shook his head and released her. "Let's go get Grace."

She didn't say anything else, just picked up the car seat and followed him to the garage where her car was parked.

Forty-five minutes later Maggie and Tucker walked back into their house with baby Grace and her belongings. On the way over and back, they both talked of other things and carefully avoided any mention of what had happened just before they left. But Tucker was damn sure not going to forget it and he didn't believe Maggie could, either. Now wasn't the time to talk about the two of them, though. Today was all about Maggie and the baby she'd wanted so badly.

"I've never seen you look this happy," Tucker said to Maggie. She'd carried the baby into the kitchen with her and didn't look like she intended to put her down for the foreseeable future.

"I'm not sure I ever have been," she said, smiling down at the baby in her arms. "No, that's not true. There was one time," she said. "But it didn't last."

"Want to talk about it?" Tucker asked.

She smiled again and shook her head. "No. Today's a happy day. I don't want to think or talk about the past." She paused and added, "But if I ever do want to talk about it, you'll be the person I talk to."

It should make him feel good that she felt she could confide in him. If she meant it. She was the most closemouthed woman he'd ever known. Beyond the few things she'd told him on their honeymoon, she hadn't said much about her past. As far as he could tell, she didn't confide in anyone. Not her parents, not her girlfriends and certainly not her husband. Was that because their marriage was a sham? Or because she looked on their relationship—their friendship, even—as temporary? Or did she just not trust him enough to confide in him?

"Is the chief okay with you taking time off work so suddenly?" Maggie had said she would take a leave of absence for a while, maybe up to several months before she went back to work.

"Yes, he was great. He's known about it so he's been prepared to deal with me suddenly leaving. He said to take as much time as I need. I told him I'd fill in occasionally when he needs someone extra. Maybe ease into part-time."

"How do you think you'll like staying home?"

"I don't know. I've worked since I was eighteen and left home, so it will be a change. But I'll have to go back sometime. I have to figure out how to work and take care of Grace since once we're divorced I'll be a single mother."

He was really beginning to hate the sound of the D word.

Grace started fussing and Maggie picked up the bottle she'd been warming. "Here you go, sweetheart," she crooned. "Let Maggie take care of you."

Tucker followed them into the other room and watched Maggie feed Grace. She'd bought a rocking chair for just that purpose. "You're going to have to teach me about child care, you know. I mean, the course was fine, but I know there are things I didn't learn. So I can keep Grace if you need to go out. Or if you go in to work."

Evidently surprised, she looked at him. "I didn't know you'd be interested."

"I have to be if you want CPS to believe we're for real."

"True. Okay, you can help me bathe her tonight. And I'll let you give her the next bottle." She watched the baby drink for a bit then said, "I keep thinking about what it will be like, staying home full-time. I've taken care of my sister's kids but just for overnights or a few hours at a time. I've never stayed home with them, not for an extended period." She shot Tucker a wry look. "Besides, I'm not exactly domestic."

"Just because you don't cook doesn't mean you're not domestic."

She laughed. "Tucker, I don't do any of the things my sister does, and she's like the ultimate stay-at-home mom. The only thing I cook is rice. Oh, and canned sweet rolls. As for cleaning, I hate it. I'd rather face an armed robber than a dirty toilet."

Tucker laughed. "So would I. That's what cleaning services are invented for."

"You should let me pay for half that, you know."

"Maggie, we've been through this before." He wasn't about to take her money, but she kept trying.

"Isn't she sweet?" Maggie asked, looking down at the baby with an expression of pure love.

"Yes, she is. And so are you."

Maggie glanced at him and smiled. "Thanks, but sweet is about the last thing people think of when they look at me."

"They don't know you, then."

She smiled again but didn't respond further.

If ever he'd seen a woman with a whole lot of love to give, it was Maggie. She held nothing back from the baby. Apparently loving the baby didn't scare her as much as the thought of loving… Whoa, why was he thinking about love? Sex on the brain was one thing, but love? They had a friendly, practical, *temporary* arrangement that didn't include sex. Love had nothing to do with the two of them.

But it could. If he wanted it to. If he was willing to risk it. Even if he was, he thought, he was fairly sure Maggie wasn't.

It was crystal clear that while the marriage was temporary to Maggie, the baby was not. What would it do to her if she lost custody of Grace?

And what would it do to him when their marriage came to an end? Could he really just walk out of Maggie's life and go on as he had before? Did he even want to?

TWO WEEKS LATER Maggie realized that being a stay-at-home mom was harder than she'd ever imagined. She loved the baby and enjoyed being with her, but taking care of Grace full-time was no easy task, she soon discovered.

If it hadn't been for Tucker, she really would have gone crazy. But he came home from work every day and spelled her, taking care of Grace so she could exercise or just relax. Plus, he talked to her, about his day or current events or sports. Whatever she wanted to talk about. She'd never been quite so isolated before. She hadn't realized she'd miss the company of adults so much.

Even better, Tucker cooked. She felt guilty since it seemed the least she could have done was try to fix something for them to eat, but it was a skill she'd never mastered. She'd tried a couple of times, but the baby would start crying or something else would happen and the next thing you knew, she'd set off the damned fire alarm again.

It didn't seem to bother Tucker. In fact, nothing seemed to bother him, not even when Grace spit up on him. Maggie didn't think he had any more experience with children than she did. Probably less since she'd at least cared for her nieces and nephew.

He was a quick study. He was almost too good to be for real. The perfect husband. Temporarily.

Maggie refused to let that thought bother her. Just as she refused to think about what would happen if they found Grace's mother. Why borrow trouble? Trouble would find her easily enough without her looking for it.

And that was why she'd tried her best to ignore what had happened when she kissed Tucker the day they brought Grace home. If they hadn't been going to get Grace… If she hadn't reminded herself that theirs was a temporary arrangement and sex did not fit in with the plan… But the fact remained, resisting Tucker was becoming harder and harder for her to do.

As she'd been doing for the past two weeks, she pushed thoughts of that kiss out of her mind and went to get Grace ready to go out when Tucker came home. He'd called earlier in the day and suggested they eat at the Scarlet Parrot that evening. She changed Grace and put her in the crib so she could take the dirty diapers out. By the time she came back, Grace had fallen asleep. Maggie let her sleep, even though it was late for a nap, since she figured they'd be out later than her bedtime, anyway.

Tucker came home a short time later while she was folding the wash on the couch. "So, how was your day?"

"It was fine." She hated folding wash, which Tucker knew because whenever he saw her folding it he helped her. "What about you? You're early."

"A little." He picked up a shirt, shook it out and folded it. "Where's Grace?"

"She's in her crib. She fell asleep after I got her dressed to go out. Why?"

"Just wondered." He folded another shirt then said, "I want to talk to you."

"Okay. Sounds serious. Is it?"

He didn't answer. He moved the basket to the floor, then made her sit beside him. She couldn't judge what he was thinking from his expression, but the longer he was quiet the more worried she grew. "Just tell me."

He gave a half laugh and rubbed the back of his neck. "I'm not sure how to do this."

"You've met someone, haven't you? Damn it, I knew this would happen."

"No. Yes." He laughed again. "I have met someone. Someone I'm very interested in. There's just one problem. She's married." She started to say something but he put his fingers on her lips before she could. "She's married to me. And I'm having a hard time asking my wife if she'd consider dating me."

She stared at him for a minute as his meaning sunk in. "We agreed—"

"I know what we agreed. How about if, just for tonight, we go out on a date? See where the evening takes us."

"This is a novel way of getting me into bed with you. I have to give you points for originality."

"I didn't ask you to go to bed with me. I asked you for a date." He smiled at her, that heart-stopping smile that always made her wonder why she was so intent on resisting him.

God, he was cute. And he'd been so sweet to her. One date wasn't a big deal, was it? *Yes, you dummy, it is. When it's a date with Tucker.* But she wavered, anyway. "We don't have a sitter."

"My parents said they'd stay with Grace."

"Your mother doesn't approve of us fostering Grace."

"My mother likes babies as much as the next woman," he said. "She's the one who suggested keeping her."

Since Eileen and Maggie had spent most of the time since the wedding avoiding each other, she hadn't known that. For the life of her she couldn't think of any more objections. She should have a million, but she wanted to go. "All right."

"Great. I'll call them."

She watched him leave the room and shook her head. A date. With her husband. What harm could there be in that?

IT HIT HER OVER the popcorn at the movie theater, so hard and so clearly she nearly stopped breathing. She was doing exactly what she'd sworn not to do. She was falling in love. With her temporary husband.

She'd come to depend on him, not only to help her with Grace but just to be there. To talk to, to argue with. To be with. A hundred times a day she'd think, *I need to tell that to Tucker when he gets home.* Something Grace did or something she saw on TV or something that occurred to her.

It had been hard enough when she'd only lusted after his body. When she'd believed he was the player he'd always seemed like on the surface, he hadn't been nearly as hard to withstand. But there was a lot more to Tucker than that, and damn it, she should have realized it before she ever conned him into marrying her.

It had to stop. Right now, before she totally blew it and did something supremely stupid. Like making love with him.

"Maggie, are you all right?"

He spoke in her ear so as not to disturb the other moviegoers, and she felt his warm breath and shivered. "I'm fine," she whispered back. "I have to go check on Grace." *You can run but you can't hide.*

"Now? It's the climax of the movie."

She just shook her head and got up, earning annoyed glares from the people she had to tromp over to get out. Who cared about a stupid movie when she was one step away from complete and total disaster?

After she called about Grace, she waited for

Tucker at the back of the theater rather than disturb everyone again by going back down the aisle. She didn't mind, it gave her some time to figure out what she was going to do.

Tucker found her when the movie let out. "Is Grace all right? I figured she must be since you didn't come get me."

"She's fine."

"Okay, then what's wrong with you?" he asked, taking her arm as they walked to the car.

"Nothing. It just occurred to me I needed to tell your mother which toy to give Grace if she couldn't get her settled. And I didn't want to disturb everyone, so I just waited."

He glanced at her as he opened the car door. "You told her that before we left. Along with leaving a list a mile long and phone numbers up the wazoo. Are you sure you're all right?"

"I'm fine, I just want to get home."

"I guess that means ice cream is out."

"Sorry. Do you mind?"

He didn't answer. After giving her a long, thoughtful look, he started the car and drove home. Once home, she checked on Grace, but the baby was sleeping soundly. She came back into the den in time to say goodbye to Tucker's parents.

Tucker shut the door behind them and walked over to her.

"It's still early. Do you want to have a drink or something?"

Oh, yeah, she needed alcohol to lower her inhibitions. "No, I think I'll turn in."

"Okay, but the date isn't officially over."

She stared at him blankly.

He put his hands on her shoulders and pulled her to him. "It's not over until you kiss me good-night."

Before she could object, or even react at all, he kissed her. His mouth was soft and knowing. His taste hot and tempting. His tongue probed her lips lightly and, heaven help her, she opened her mouth and drew him in even though her mind screamed *mistake*. This was exactly what she'd been desperately trying to avoid ever since she'd kissed him the day they brought Grace home. He kissed her slowly, lingering, making her breasts tingle and her legs weak. Making her head spin, making her wish...

If he can do that to me with a kiss, what would going to bed with him be like?

Wonderful. And too damn risky.

Maggie jerked back. "We need to talk."

He smiled at her and released her. "What do you want to talk about, Maggie?"

"Divorce."

CHAPTER THIRTEEN

"YOU WANT A DIVORCE because I kissed you good-night? Don't you think that's a little dramatic?" Especially since she'd been as involved in that kiss as he was. What was going on in that gorgeous head of hers?

She had paced away, but at his question she turned to face him. "Don't be ridiculous. I just think it's time we talked about the divorce. Now that I have Grace."

"*We* are Grace's foster parents," he reminded her. "You said you wanted to adopt her."

"I do, but I don't know when I'll be able to do that. It could be a long time."

"Yeah, I knew that when I signed on. The original plan was to stay married until we found out about adopting Grace."

"Plans can change. I think we should discuss divorce."

This made no sense. What had spooked her to

the point that she suddenly wanted a divorce? He stared at her, and then it dawned on him what was happening. "You're scared. I kissed you and it was good and now you're freaking out."

"You're putting way too much importance on a kiss. That has nothing to do with talking about divorce."

"Doesn't it? We're getting closer and it scares you. To the point that to keep me at arm's length, you bring up divorce."

"I'm not scared of you. I'm a cop; I'm not scared of anything."

"Oh, baby, you are so scared you don't know what to do. But not of me. Of yourself. Of your emotions."

She gave him a pitying look. "If it makes you feel better to think so, you go right ahead."

She put a good face on it, he'd give her that. But he hadn't imagined her response. Or the fact that every time they grew closer she reacted by putting as much space between them as she could. So he went to her, stood right smack in her personal space, and lowered his voice. "You weren't so cool a minute ago. When you were melting in my arms like warm honey."

"Please." She rolled her eyes. "I won't deny I enjoyed kissing you. So what? I'm a normal woman with normal feelings. But melting? In your dreams."

She had that right. He'd been dreaming about her for weeks now. She played in his head like a picture in HDTV, vivid and so real you could reach out and touch it. And he was tired of resisting, tired of pretending he only wanted her as a friend. "Prove it. If that kiss was nothing to you then kiss me again."

"No," she said abruptly, and moved back. "We need to work on putting distance between us. All this—this…cozying up has got to stop. Being close will just make things that much harder when we divorce."

"That's a pretty weak excuse, Maggie. I still think you're scared."

"I'm not scared, I'm being practical."

"So practical you won't even give us a chance." What would it take to get through to her? And why did he keep beating his head against this particular wall? He could have other women, just as soon as they divorced.

But he didn't want other women. He wanted Maggie. The woman who had married him and then spent every moment pushing him as far away as she possibly could. Rational or not, it pissed him off.

"Fine. You want distance, that's just what you'll get." He turned on his heel and left, knowing sleep was going to be impossible to come by that night. He was too mad. And too…hurt, damn it.

She didn't trust him. She'd married him, but only because she thought he would be easy to divorce. If she'd thought there was any potential of a real relationship, she would never have married him. She had never had any intention of having a lasting relationship with him. What's more, she'd been up front about that from the beginning. And he, God help him, had agreed. He'd been so sure that all he felt for Maggie was friendship, and maybe in the beginning that had been true.

But it sure as hell wasn't true now.

"ARE YOU STILL MAD at me?" Maggie asked Tucker a little more than a week later.

He glanced at her, then back to the road. They were headed home from his parents' house, after attending a surprise party for his father's birthday.

"I'm not mad at you."

He'd gotten past the anger, but he wasn't happy, either. The conviction had been growing over the past few weeks that he knew just exactly what it was going to take to make him really happy. And he was fairly certain he wasn't going to get it.

"Right. You're not a bit mad. That's why you've hardly spoken to me in a week."

He shrugged. "Just giving you distance, babe. I thought that's what you wanted."

"I did, too. But…I didn't want you to be so angry with me. Maybe…maybe I was wrong when I said we shouldn't be close. I mean, we are still living together."

Still living together. And it seemed to him she was counting every moment until she could divorce him. Okay, he'd lied. He was still angry, damned angry, and he knew he had no right to be. He'd agreed to this crazy scheme of Maggie's. He'd agreed to marry her and live with her and not have sex with her. No one had held a gun to his head. Worse, he couldn't even say it was all about the sex, or the lack of it. It wasn't Maggie's fault that he was… Shit, he wasn't falling, he'd flat fallen in love with her.

"Tucker, I didn't mean to hurt you," she said, sounding troubled. "That's the last thing I want to do."

She had hurt him, whether she'd intended to

or not. But no good would come of admitting that. "You didn't hurt me. Forget it, okay?"

"Can we at least go back to being friends? I miss you."

He glanced at her. Damn, he wished she didn't get to him. He wished he could go back to being just friends…but it was way too late for him. "Sure. And Maggie?" He waited until she looked at him. "For the record, I missed you, too." She gave her quick grin but didn't add anything.

He was quiet a moment, then changed the subject. "What did my mother want when she dragged you off with her?"

Maggie laughed. "I felt sorry for her. I think your mother's trying to teach me some culture. She introduced me to a lot of women on that opera committee of hers and talked about me joining. I didn't know how to tactfully tell her I'd rather bite off my hand than be on a committee like that."

"How did you get out of it?"

"I lied, sort of. I let her think I was going back to work sooner than I am. And I told her between my job and Grace I just didn't have the time. She didn't say anything else, but she can sure look disapproving."

"She'll get over it."

"I hope so. The redhead you were talking to while I was trapped with your mother? That was Isabella, wasn't it? I had to wonder if your mother strategically arranged that. Making sure you know what you're missing, you know."

"I haven't missed anything."

"Really?" She was quiet a moment, then asked, "You don't miss being with other women? Not even a little?"

"Have I complained?"

"No, but that doesn't mean you don't miss it. Most men would."

Tucker pulled into the driveway and put the car in Park. "What's going on? Did my mother say something to upset you?"

"It's nothing. I'll go get the babysitter and pay her. Do you mind driving her home or do you want me to?"

"I'll do it. I'll just wait in the car."

He watched her go inside. Something was definitely up with her. He hoped his mother hadn't been responsible for upsetting her. Since their talk before the wedding, Eileen had treated Maggie much better. At least, Maggie hadn't let on if she hadn't. But Tucker knew his mother still thought the marriage was ill-advised.

After he took the babysitter home he parked

in the garage and came in through the kitchen. He found Maggie in the den, dressed in her favorite sleepwear, a tank top and shorts. He sighed, refusing to be distracted, though he found her just as appealing now as he had earlier when she'd been dressed up for the party. Not that it mattered. Besides, right now he wanted to know what had happened between Maggie and his mother.

"What did my mother say to you? And don't lie and tell me it's nothing."

"She didn't say anything, exactly. It's just… She hasn't come right out and said it, but it's pretty clear she thinks I'm the worst sort of wife for you."

"Why is that?" He took a seat on the couch, watching Maggie as she paced.

She stopped and turned to him. "Come on, Tucker. I'm nothing like the women you used to date. I'm not beautiful and poised and… whatever. I'm not into society. I don't like any of the things those women do."

"First of all, you are beautiful. Second of all, not every woman I ever dated was a socialite. Regardless of what my mother thinks, I dated a variety of women."

"Maybe, but I'm about as far from your

mother's vision of the ideal woman for you as it's possible to get."

"Why are you so obsessed with what my mother thinks?"

"I don't know. I know it shouldn't get to me, but it does. It makes me feel, I don't know, inadequate."

"Well, you're not. Who cares what she thinks? You'll notice I didn't marry any of those women."

"You didn't marry me, either. Not for real."

He got up and walked over to her. "It feels pretty real to me. We live together. We have a baby to care for." He reached out and touched her hair, let the silky strands slip through his fingers. "We talk. We argue. We eat meals together. We work out together. The only thing we don't do that people in a real marriage do is make love." He moved even closer, leaned in and kissed her cheek, slid his lips along her skin to the corner of her mouth and kissed her there. "We could change that."

"Tucker—" She sighed but she didn't resist when he put his arms around her and pulled her even closer. "You're confusing me and I don't like—" He heard her breath catch as his lips cruised her jawline.

"What don't you like, Maggie?" He slid his

hands up her waist to just under her breasts, flicked his thumbs over her nipples. "This?" She didn't say anything, just looked at him, her eyes huge and dark. "Or this?" Giving in to the urge he'd been fighting for so long, he cupped her breasts through the thin, silky fabric of her tank. Massaged her with his palms and wondered what it would feel like to touch her even softer bare skin.

Her lips were parted and her breath was coming harder but still she didn't stop him. "We shouldn't," she said. "But you're making it hard for me to remember why."

"Kiss me, Maggie. Don't analyze, don't think. Just kiss me."

She wrapped her arms around his neck and kissed him. She kissed like a fantasy. And she tasted like a dream. Sweet, with a hot, sexy taste beneath it.

Instead of devouring her as he was tempted to do, he let his tongue search her mouth, explore it, thrust and withdraw until her tongue answered his in a deep, stirring, sensual kiss. Long moments later, he raised his head and smiled at her.

Her mouth curved upward, too. "I'm not sure I care if this is a mistake."

"It's not. Trust me, it's not." She was warm and giving and he marveled that a woman as strong and capable as he knew Maggie to be could also be so soft and inviting.

Keeping his eyes on hers, he pushed up her tank and stroked bare skin. Her skin was like silk. He kissed her again, walking her backward until her knees hit the couch, then followed her down. He stopped kissing her long enough to push up her tank and draw it off over her head.

For a long moment he simply gazed at her, dry-mouthed.

"You're just as beautiful as I've imagined." Her breasts were full and lush, with tight coral tips that just begged to be kissed. He intended to give them a very thorough inspection. He touched his tongue to a peak, licked it, then very slowly, sucked it into his mouth.

Maggie moaned and put her hands in his hair. "Oh, that feels so good…don't stop."

"Wouldn't dream of it," he said, taking her other breast in his mouth. He sucked her nipple, tongued it. She leaned back against his arm, completely bare from the waist up, and Tucker drew in his breath in rapt appreciation. Smooth, creamy white skin, gorgeous breasts, her red hair spilling over her shoulders inviting him to do things he'd been fantasizing about for weeks, for months.

"Incredible," he said, and went to work again. Soon, she squirmed against him, arching her back to push her breasts into his mouth. He suckled first one, then the other, drawing the tight peaks into his mouth and tormenting them both, using his fingers on the one his mouth had just left.

She moaned again when he slipped his hand down to her shorts and slid his fingers between her legs to touch her through the skimpy fabric.

"Tucker…" She said his name on a sigh as he skimmed his fingers over her again. She was damp with anticipation and it took all of his willpower not to strip those shorts off that instant and plunge inside her.

"Let's get rid of these." He started to tug her shorts down but Maggie put her hand on his wrist.

"Uh-uh," she said huskily. "First you have to lose the shirt."

"You do it," he told her.

She sat up a little and reached for the buttons, keeping her eyes on his as she opened them one by one. When she reached the waistband of his pants, she tugged the shirt free. Then she pushed the shirt down his arms and looked at him. She put her hands on him, slid them over his chest and nipples, then raised her eyes to meet his. The smile that curved her mouth was pure sin.

Her eyes had changed color and were now almost turquoise as she concentrated on him, stroking his chest with a light, deft touch. His nipples tightened and she moved closer and kissed his neck, then nipped it. Tucker groaned.

He cupped her and she moaned and pushed herself against his hand. She lay down on the couch and he followed, ending up between silky thighs. He rocked against her and she tightened her arms and legs around him. Nuzzling her neck, he asked, "Why are we on the couch when we have a nice, comfortable bed we could be in?"

"Because," she said as she ran her hands down his back to his butt and pulled him against her again. "I'm still not sure we should be doing this."

"I have to tell you, you're not acting like you're thinking this is a mistake."

She sighed. "You're right, I'm not."

He kissed her mouth again, slowly, then drew back and smiled at her. "Have I told you recently that you're beautiful?"

She laughed, the sound a sexy ripple, before

her expression grew solemn. "I want you, Tucker. Inside me."

A cell phone rang. He glanced at the coffee table. "That's yours. Don't answer it."

She looked undecided. "It might be important."

"So is this."

"Tucker, I have to answer it."

Reluctantly, he moved off her and she sat up and reached for the phone, grabbing for her tank with her other hand and holding it against her chest. "I'm sorry," she said, then picked up the phone and flipped it open.

"Hello." She paused and said, "Yes, this is Officer Barnes." She paused then said, "Sara? Sara Myers?"

He watched her change from disheveled, about-to-be-thoroughly loved woman to pure cop in an instant.

"No, don't do that. It's too dangerous. Keep that door locked and I'll be there as soon as I can. Don't open the door, Sara, until you hear me or another officer. I'm on my way now."

She shut the cell phone with a snap, and yanked her tank top over her head and down to cover her breasts. "Shit, I knew this was going to happen. Tucker, I have to go." She jumped up and headed for the bedroom.

"What's wrong?" He followed her, watching as she rifled through her closet for her uniform and then scrambled into it.

"Remember that domestic disturbance I was called to the day I found Grace? The last time I pulled you over? I left the woman my number. I don't always, but I had a feeling about her.

"I was right. She just called. Husband's out of control again. She's had to lock herself in her bedroom to get away from him. He's already broken her nose. Now he's threatened to break every bone in her body if she doesn't let him in."

"Are you going to call for backup? You're not even working. You're on a leave of absence still. Maybe someone else should take the call." He wished she wouldn't go at all, but he knew she would.

"No, she's mine. She trusted me and she called me. Besides, I told you, I'm a cop. I'm always on duty. I'll call the station on the way." She strapped on her belt and added the gun. "With any luck I'll be able to arrest the bastard this time around. Last time she wouldn't let us press charges. Denied he ever touched her."

He walked with her into the kitchen. "Call me and let me know you're okay," he told her.

Maybe he was overreacting but he had a bad feeling about this situation.

She smiled as she shrugged into her jacket. "Don't worry, Tucker. I do this kind of thing all the time."

He knew she did. That didn't mean he had to like it. "Just be careful."

"Always." She paused a moment before she left. "Tucker, about tonight...I'm sorry."

A moment later she was gone. And Tucker was alone with only a sleeping baby and a nagging fear for Maggie for company.

CHAPTER FOURTEEN

MAGGIE AND A FELLOW officer named Ben Fair-field arrived at the apartment building at almost the same time. Ben had only been with the ACPD for a few months but Maggie had worked with him before and liked him.

"Glad you made it," Maggie told him.

Nodding, he said, "I thought you were on leave."

"I was. I am, but the victim called me and said she was locked in the bedroom with her husband threatening to break every bone in her body. Said he's already broken her nose, so he might just mean it."

Ben nodded again. "Apartment 3-D, you say."

"That's right. Third floor."

"Is he armed?"

"I don't know." Maggie glanced at the building with a worried frown. "She didn't say he had a gun, but that doesn't mean anything.

She was scared out of her mind and might not have thought to mention it."

"One way to find out," Ben said. "Let's go."

A few minutes later Maggie pounded on the door. "Police, open up."

"I'm glad you're here. I think he may have killed her this time."

Maggie turned around to see a woman peering out of the apartment across the hall. "Why do you say that?"

"There was a lot of noise, hollering and cursing. Then it got quiet before starting again, even worse. He was throwing things around, from the sound of it. I think maybe she was one of the things he threw." She nodded, her face grim. "There was a huge crash and since then, nothing."

"Did you hear any gunshots?" Ben asked the woman.

"No, but I know he keeps a gun. Sara told me one time she was afraid the children would find it." She paused and added, "I called the police before on this man but you've never done anything."

Maggie stifled a pang of regret. *I tried*, she thought, but it hadn't been good enough. "Thanks for your help," she said and waited until the woman closed her door before pounding on Sara's again. "Aransas City Police Department. Open the door." She tried the knob, but it was locked.

Still no answer. She and Ben exchanged a glance. She took out her weapon and so did he. At her nod, he kicked in the door and entered the apartment with Maggie right behind him.

The place was a shambles, with broken dishes everywhere and a good bit of the furniture broken, as well. Apparently, he'd put one of the chairs through the TV screen. There was no sign of any people. The doors to both bedrooms were shut and there was an ominous silence. "Police," she called out.

Maggie pointed at the door of what she knew from her previous visit was the master bedroom. She and Ben flanked it on either side. "Sara, can you hear me? Are you all right?"

A bullet came through the door and buried itself in the wall across the hall. They heard a wild laugh, then a man said, "She won't answer. The bitch got what she deserved."

Maggie's heart sank. Although she hadn't relished a standoff, at least that would have meant Sara had a chance. She nodded at Ben, for him to try again before they went in. Maybe the man was lying. Maybe—

"Sara Myers, are you all right?"

Another bullet through the door was their only answer. Ben counted to three with his fingers in the air and on three Maggie turned the knob and pushed the door open. Seconds later several shots rang out, though they all went wild and didn't hit either of them.

"Police! Put down your weapon," Ben shouted.

"That'll be a cold day in hell. Come and take it," the man invited. "That bitch won't be calling the cops no more."

Maggie went in low and Ben high, both of them aiming for the place they'd last heard the man's voice. Several shots sounded and Maggie jerked back, feeling a searing pain in her arm. "Shit, he hit me."

Ben didn't answer but she couldn't look at him until she made sure the shooter was taken care of. He'd been hit, that much was obvious, and he lay slumped over. Holding her gun on him, she walked over to him and checked his pulse. "Dead." A small arsenal of handguns surrounded him, yet by some miracle, they'd taken him out before he took them. She turned and looked for her partner, who lay on the floor, bleeding. "Damn it, you're hurt! Why didn't you say something? How did he hit both of us?" She rushed over to him.

"Just lucky, I guess," he said, grimacing. "He got my shoulder, but I don't think it's bad."

"No, I don't, either," Maggie said, inspecting it. She keyed in her radio. "Officer down! Officer needs assistance!" Then she went into the bathroom and grabbed a couple of towels, wadding one up to hold over Ben's wound.

He was hurt more than he let on because he allowed her to staunch the blood without arguing, which was totally unlike the man she'd worked with before. "You're bleeding, too," he said, a little faintly.

"It's just a flesh wound. I'll survive." And so would Ben, she thought, looking him over critically.

"Who do you think got him?"

"I don't know. Maybe you." She glanced around and caught sight of the very still form of Sara Myers, lying beside the dresser.

"Go to her," Ben said, brushing her hands aside to hold the towel. "I'm all right."

She was sure they were too late but she went to her, anyway. Sara looked…broken. She searched for a pulse but couldn't find it. She closed her eyes, hung her head and sucked in a breath. She looked at Ben. "She's dead. No gunshot wound. I think her neck's broken."

"Bastard probably did it when he threw her," Ben said. "You're bleeding like a stuck pig," he added. "Better put some pressure on that."

Maggie didn't argue. At least she was alive, unlike poor Sara Myers.

"We were too late. I wonder when he did it. If I'd gotten here faster…" She shook her head, then sat on the floor before she fell down.

"Don't beat yourself up," Ben advised.

She just shook her head, gazing at the dead woman.

"Maggie, don't take it so hard. We did the best we could."

"Yeah, I know. But it wasn't good enough." She'd failed, just as she'd failed weeks earlier to talk Sara into going to a shelter. And now Sara Myers was dead. There would be no chances of a new life for her.

THE HOUSE WAS QUIET when she returned, much later. She hoped Tucker had gone to sleep. After she left the hospital, where the doctors had assured them Ben would recover fully, she went to the station and called to tell him she was all right, but that she'd be a while and for him not to wait up. She hadn't told him about being shot or that her partner had been shot, as well. She figured she'd better tell him that in person. She wasn't too sure of his reaction, but she didn't think it would be good.

After putting her weapon and belt away, she checked on Grace but the baby was sleeping peacefully. So sweet, so peaceful, she thought, stifling the urge to pick her up and cuddle her for comfort. Instead she left her and went back to the den.

Going straight to the bar, she found a bottle of whiskey and picked up a glass. She splashed some liquor in it and tossed it back, shuddering as it burned its way down. Maggie didn't drink a lot, but she knew why so many cops did. Tonight was one of those nights when she could easily have crawled inside a bottle. She wouldn't, but she sure as hell intended to have a drink. Or two or three.

Her arm throbbed and she wondered if she'd been stupid not to take the prescription pain meds she'd been offered. Probably, but she'd decided to make do with over-the-counter pills and have a drink instead.

"I listened to the police scanner," Tucker said

from the doorway. "I heard them say officer down. They didn't even have to specify, I knew it was you."

"It wasn't me. It was my partner." She gripped the glass tighter and downed another swallow. "He's going to be okay, though." Keeping her injured arm turned away from him, she glanced at him. "You shouldn't listen to the scanner. Especially if I'm gone."

"Right, that's going to happen. Looks like you had a rough night."

"Yeah." She laughed without humor and took another sip of whiskey. "It totally blew wide out."

He walked over to her, picked up the bottle and poured her some more. "Come sit down." He started to take her by the arm, then frowned, obviously noticing the bandage on her other arm for the first time. "I thought you said your partner was shot. What happened to your arm?" He rubbed her bare skin below the bandage gently. "You were shot, too, weren't you? Goddamn it, Maggie, you've been shot! Why didn't you tell me when you called?"

Maggie cursed herself. It looked worse than it was, she knew. They'd had to cut off her shirt-sleeve to put a bandage the size of Aransas Bay on her arm.

"It's nothing. Just a flesh wound."

"Nothing? You were shot. That's a long way from nothing. I can't believe you didn't tell me. I'd have come to the hospital with you."

"And what would you have done with Grace? Besides, I didn't tell you because I didn't want you to freak out like you're doing now." She let him lead her to the couch and sat down.

"I'm not freaking out. But, yes, it upsets me to know that my wife has been shot and didn't bother to tell me." He sat beside her.

"I'm sorry." She set her glass down and rubbed a hand over her forehead. "I thought it would be better to tell you in person. Maybe I was wrong, I don't know."

"Tell me what happened."

She gazed at him before she began. He had that implacable look on his face. He wouldn't be put off this time, she knew. Besides, she wanted to talk to him. He was bare-chested, wearing only a pair of thin sweats that he must have pulled on when he heard her come in. He looked warm and strong and infinitely comforting. Tears stung her eyes and she resolutely fought them back. *Suck it up,* she told herself. *You're tough, you're a cop. Pull it together.* She took another drink before she started.

"He was holed up in the apartment with a small arsenal, but we didn't know that. We weren't even sure he was armed. Neighbor heard a lot of commotion, then nothing. We called out to the victim but she didn't answer." She skipped over the part about all the shooting, figuring the less Tucker heard about that the better. "We believe she was dead by the time we got there. The son of a bitch she was married to broke her neck. He threw her into the dresser. Like…like she was nothing."

Tucker put his hand over hers and squeezed comfortingly. "I'm sorry. I can't imagine how hard it must be for you to walk into that kind of a situation."

She shrugged, then winced at the jolt of pain. "At least I'm alive. Sara Myers is dead. And it's my fault."

CHAPTER FIFTEEN

TUCKER STARED AT HER. She was serious. "Maggie, it's foolish to blame yourself for this." She didn't say anything. He didn't think she'd even heard him, she was so caught up in her grief and guilt. "What happened to him? Is he in jail? I'm assuming he's the one who shot you and your partner."

She nodded. "Yeah. He's not in jail. He's dead. Ben Fairfield shot and killed him but not before he'd managed to shoot both of us. At least, we think it was Ben's shot and not mine that got him."

"You could have been killed." Maybe it wasn't what she needed to hear, but it made him sick to think how close she'd come to— He shook his head, not wanting that thought in it. He knew the dangers of police work. Hell, anyone who watched the news knew them. It was just different when it was personal, when it affected someone you cared about. When it affected his wife.

"It's nothing. I got lucky. Sara Myers didn't."

"Why do you feel so responsible for her?"

"Because she trusted me. Because I couldn't get her into a shelter where she could get help." She got up and started pacing. Tucker could sense the frustration coming off her in waves. "I tried everything I could think of to get her to a shelter, but she wouldn't buy it. She was so damn sure he was a good guy underneath it all. I failed to convince her of the danger and now she's dead."

"Maggie, you can't possibly blame yourself over every case or every call that goes south. You'd be crazy by now. You couldn't function as a cop. So why are you letting this particular one get to you so badly?"

"I don't know." She rubbed a hand over her eyes. "No, that's a lie. I know exactly why she gets to me. Why this whole miserable situation gets to me."

"Tell me."

She came back and sat beside him, picked up her nearly empty glass and drained it.

"Do you want more?"

She shot him a look he couldn't interpret,

then shook her head before setting down the empty glass. "I don't usually drink when something bad happens. I've known too many cops who slid inside a bottle and couldn't seem to make it out. But tonight… God, talk about ghosts of the past." She was quiet for a long moment, then she began.

"I met him for the first time when we went out on a domestic disturbance call."

"Met who?" he asked, but he had a feeling he knew.

"Spencer Whitman." She laughed bitterly. "The love of my life. I was in Dallas. It was my first call with the department and they gave me to him. He'd been around several years longer than I had and he had a rep for being a negotiator. He could talk anyone into anything. If we had a jumper, say, and couldn't find a shrink, he'd be the guy everyone wanted to talk him down." She smiled. "He really had a golden tongue."

"Were you partners?"

She nodded. "Eventually. That first time, I was just a rookie, following him around. Anyway, we went to a domestic disturbance. Almost exactly the same scenario as the one I walked into the night I found Grace. Sara Myers even looked a bit like that woman. But Spencer was able to talk the woman into going to a shelter. It was amazing, how he convinced her."

"And you feel like you should have been able to convince Sara Myers just because he got lucky that one time."

"It wasn't luck, or just an isolated incident. He had a gift. I saw him do it, time after time. And I learned from him, or thought I had. I've had a good success rate in these kind of situations until now."

"Maggie, it was Sara Myers's choice to stay with her abuser. None of this is your failure."

"You're wrong. My failure killed Sara." She put her head in her hands, then looked at him with tormented eyes. "My God, Tucker, I turned her into a sitting duck. I should have told her to run."

"And that could have turned out just as badly. Or even worse if other people had been hurt. You don't have a crystal ball. You can't say that if you'd done or said something different you could have saved her. As it was, both you and your partner were shot. One or both of you could have been killed. Or any number of innocent bystanders could have been hurt if the man hadn't been contained to that apartment."

She looked unconvinced.

"Did they have kids?"

Maggie nodded. "Three. They were huddled in the other bedroom, terrified to make a sound in case it reminded their father they were there. CPS has them now."

"At least the children weren't hurt. Can't you take any comfort from that?"

"Some." She frowned at him. "Okay, a lot. But I still hate that it turned out this way. I hate that she's dead and I couldn't stop him."

"I can understand that. But I don't understand why it reminds you so much of your past. Of Spencer."

She got up and walked back over to the bar, but she didn't pick up the whiskey bottle. Her shoulders squared and she turned back to him. "I don't know, exactly. It's like they're connected in my mind. I think failure connects them. Whenever I fail, especially if it's a domestic disturbance case, I think about Spencer. I feel inadequate again. Just like I felt with your mother earlier. I'm not good enough for your mother. I wasn't good enough to save Sara. And I wasn't good enough to make Spencer fall in love with me. No matter how much I loved him."

He'd thought he wanted to hear the story. Now he wasn't so sure. "Maggie, come sit down." He didn't care how minor she said the wound was, she'd been shot. She ought to be in bed, but barring that, she should at least sit down.

She crossed the room and sat beside him again. "I fell for him. Completely, madly in love. We had an affair. A red-hot affair that lasted about eight months."

"I thought cops weren't supposed to get involved with their partners."

"Technically they're not. In reality it happens all the time."

"Was he in love with you?"

"No." She shook her head, quick and decisive. "No, he never told me he loved me. Never lied to me or tried to make me believe what we had was anything more to him than something to keep the loneliness at bay. He cared about me, I know he did. And he liked the sex, but he didn't love me."

So big deal, the guy hadn't lied to her. He'd used her. And obviously, he'd hurt her. Tucker wished for just a few minutes alone with the man.

"I knew he was hung up on another woman, but I was so damn sure I could make him fall for me instead. She was the only person I ever knew of who Spencer couldn't convince to do what he wanted. He wanted her to leave her husband for him. She refused, said she wanted to save her marriage, so she and Spencer couldn't see each other anymore. They'd only been broken up a month or so when I met him."

"He hurt you. Badly."

"More like I hurt myself by not seeing reality. Then I got pregnant. I was so happy. I had all the fantasies that, once he knew, Spencer would marry me and the three of us would live happily ever after." She gave a short, bitter laugh. "We were both off duty and I went to tell him about the baby. But I found him packing. He said he'd been planning to tell me that evening. He was leaving Dallas. Seems he'd finally talked the woman he loved into leaving her husband and they were going to start fresh somewhere else. So, bye-bye, Maggie, it's been nice knowing you."

"Bastard."

"No, he wasn't." She shook her head. "Don't blame him for my problems. He didn't know I loved him. I never told him. And I knew all along he was in love with another woman. I just didn't want to admit I couldn't change his mind and make him fall for me. But you can't make someone love you. I learned that the hard way."

Tucker had a bad feeling he was going to have to learn the hard way, as well.

"Did you ever tell him you were pregnant?"

"No. I didn't see the point. It wouldn't have changed anything. I figured a baby with me would just ruin his life and he'd finally gotten what—who—he wanted. So I left Dallas and came back to Aransas City. I...wanted to be near family. I thought it would be better since I was going to be a single mother."

Tucker remembered when she'd said she'd needed her mother, and her mother hadn't been there for her. "What happened to the baby?"

Her expression was bleak. Her eyes huge and full of pain. "I had a miscarriage, not long after I came back. I told the chief I was pregnant but no one else knew. I thought I'd wait until I started showing. I never reached that stage."

He took her hand and squeezed it. "I'm so sorry, Maggie. You wanted it, didn't you?"

"Yeah, I wanted the baby. More than I'd ever wanted anything. The doctor said it was just one of those things. Nothing I did to cause it, nothing I could have done to prevent it. But I've always wondered...."

"Wondered what? That you were at fault?"

She started to shrug, then caught herself, wincing. "Maybe. I always wondered if the miscarriage was payback."

"Payback for what?"

"Remember my affair with the married man? The married man with the pregnant wife?"

Tucker just stared at her. She couldn't possibly believe what she was implying, could she? "Maggie, that's crazy. The whole situation was much more his fault than yours. He lied to you, told you he was legally separated. Besides, it's not like there's some kind of cosmic karma that says, 'Oh, Maggie screwed up so we're going to take her baby away from her.'"

"It was as good an explanation as the one I got from the doctor."

"Have you ever talked to anyone about this?"

"No. What would have been the point? I had a miscarriage. Wham, bam, no more baby. It was over and done with and I moved on."

But had she moved on? Suddenly her reasons for wanting to keep Grace became much clearer. As well as her fear of intimacy. At least two of the men she'd been intimate with had screwed her over royally. No wonder she didn't trust men.

"I know what you're thinking," Maggie said. "Grace isn't a substitute for the baby I lost. I feel a connection with her, that's all."

He didn't know what to say to her. How to comfort her. Because she needed comforting, no matter how much she believed she didn't. So he didn't say anything. Not yet. Careful not to jar her injury, he urged her closer and put his arm around her. "I'm sorry. I wish someone had been there for you when you lost the baby."

She put her uninjured arm around his neck and sighed, leaning against him. "Why are you so nice to me? You're always so nice. So understanding."

Because I'm in love with you, he thought. But there was no way he could tell her that. He'd only begun to admit it to himself. She wasn't ready to hear how he felt. Maybe she never would be.

"You deserve someone to be nice to you," he said lightly. "And you also need someone to put you to bed, since you won't go yourself. You're exhausted, Maggie. You need to get some sleep."

"I know." She sighed. "I shouldn't have drunk that whiskey on an empty stomach. I don't feel so good. And now if Grace wakes up— I'm just batting a thousand tonight for doing the wrong thing."

"I'll take care of Grace if she needs anything." And he intended to take care of Maggie, too. "Come on, I'll make you some scrambled eggs."

She sat at the kitchen table and watched him prepare the eggs, not saying anything. But her eyes were stricken and he knew she was replaying the events of the night in her mind. Torturing herself with what-ifs.

He put the plate in front of her. "Eat."

While she ate he steered the conversation to Grace, and what she'd done that day, and had the satisfaction of seeing the desperate look slowly leave Maggie's eyes as she talked about the baby and that she could now sit up. A milestone, Maggie said, and he'd even managed to snap a picture.

"I don't know why I'm so tired," Maggie said, laying down her fork. She'd eaten a little, though not as much as he'd have liked. At least she had some color back, but she looked exhausted still.

"It might have something to do with being shot." He led her to her bedroom, ignoring her when she tried to thank him and get rid of him. No way was he leaving her alone with her memories. Not tonight.

He picked up the tank top she'd thrown on the chair. "Can you get into this by yourself or do you need help?"

She took it from him. "Tucker, I'm fine. You don't have to baby me."

"Would you for once listen to me? Get undressed and get into bed."

He knew how exhausted she was because she didn't argue. She simply stripped out of her uniform where she stood and pulled on her tank and shorts. Then she crawled into bed. He got into bed with her, on top of the covers, with her uninjured arm against him. "Don't even try to argue with me," he told her.

"I won't. I should, but…I'm glad you're here." She snuggled against him, laying her poor injured arm over his chest.

"Yeah, me, too. Go to sleep, Maggie." She dropped off soon after, and just as he'd expected, she woke in pain, with a nightmare, deep in the night. Tucker gave her aspirin, then he held her, comforted her until she calmed down.

And his heart twisted when she said sleepily against him, "Tucker, you're my best friend," before she dropped off to sleep again.

She needed a friend, and he was happy to be there for her. But he wanted more, as well. A whole hell of a lot more. Because he'd finally admitted tonight, when he heard the chilling words "officer down" come over the police scanner and known it could be Maggie, what he'd tried to ignore for weeks now. He was totally, madly and, in all probability, hopelessly in love with his wife.

CHAPTER SIXTEEN

MAGGIE WOKE EARLY the next morning, aware that her arm was throbbing and that her head rested on a warm, hard, masculine chest. Tucker's chest. She sat up suddenly, then had to bite her lip to keep from screaming at the dizzying rush of pain. Whoever had said flesh wounds weren't a big deal had obviously never had one. As she gazed at him, Tucker's eyes opened and he smiled at her sleepily.

"Hey."

"Hey yourself," she said, smiling in spite of the pain.

"How's your arm?"

His voice was a deep rumble, rough with sleep. He looked as good as he sounded, all rumpled and sexy with his morning beard and those beautiful deep-water-blue eyes smiling at her.

"You didn't have to stay with me." She sounded ungracious, but damn, she'd been dreaming about him—sexy, sensual dreams, and then to wake in his arms… Still, no wonder she was a little shaken. The sexy dreams beat the hell out of the other dreams she'd had.

"You had a nightmare," he said, then rolled on his side and propped himself on one arm. "Which isn't a surprise, considering."

The night before came back in a flood of memories. She and Tucker, about to make love. Then the call. The whole futile scene at the apartment. Sara Myers, dead. And when she'd come back home…

God, she'd told Tucker her whole miserable history with Spencer. How much had she drunk? And what in the world was the matter with her to spill her guts like she had? She never did that. Never. But then, for some reason Tucker caused her to do a whole lot of stupid things she didn't usually do.

She got out of bed, careful not to jar her arm any more than she had to. "Yeah, I remember. But you didn't need to sleep with me."

"Trust me, Maggie, it wasn't a hardship." He looked amused. And tempting. He'd gotten under the covers at some point the night before and now the sheet pooled around his waist. She tried not to look at his bare chest, to see the ripple of muscles as he got up and stretched. But that was impossible.

She took the coward's way out and dashed into the bathroom. He was gone when she emerged a few minutes later and she breathed a sigh of relief. Grabbing her rattiest, oldest robe, she went to get Grace and found Tucker there before her, talking to the baby while he finished changing her diaper.

"That's right, Gracie. Tucker's going to give you a bottle and then we're going to check out the newspaper."

Her heart simply melted. God, they were cute together. Grace was kicking her feet and babbling that strange language only babies understand. Tucker had put on a plain white T-shirt and he looked…like a father taking care of his child, she realized with a pang of longing. Oh, damn, she had to stop this. "I'll take her if you want me to."

He glanced over at her and smiled, then put the baby against his shoulder and walked to the door. Grace peeped at her over Tucker's shoulder, all blond curly hair, big blue eyes and sweet as only babies can be. "I don't think so. Have you tried to pick up anything heavy?"

Maggie frowned. "I can manage. Besides,

you're going to work, so you might as well let me have her." She reached out for her and sucked in a breath, then cradled her arm against her side. Okay, so taking care of Grace wouldn't be easy, but she could still do it.

Ignoring her, Tucker carried Grace into the kitchen and fixed her bottle of formula, then set out the cereal to give her when she finished. It annoyed Maggie that he was already at least as competent as she in caring for the baby.

"I'm taking a couple of days off work," Tucker said. "I already called Janice and told her to reschedule, so don't argue."

"You don't need to do that. I can take care of Grace." Maybe.

"Didn't I say don't argue? You'll have to go in to finish your report. And you'll have to talk to a lot of other people if they determine your shot killed that man, won't you?"

"Ben and I both think it was his. Anyway, what do you know about what happens when you shoot someone?"

"Just what I see on TV. But it's true, isn't it?" She didn't answer and he continued, "So let me take care of Grace while you deal with your business."

He'd left her with nothing to say or do, which

irritated the heck out of her. She stalked over to the phone to call the hospital for an update on Ben's condition. Even though she'd expected good news or she wouldn't have left the night before, she still breathed a huge sigh of relief to hear they would release him later that day.

For the next few days, she and Tucker played house. At least, that's how Maggie tried to look at it. Because she sure couldn't afford to look on those days together, as a family, as something real.

SCHEMING HOW TO SEDUCE his own wife was more difficult than Tucker would have thought. He hadn't said anything or made a move since she'd been shot. First because she'd been hurt, and later because he wasn't sure how to approach her. He'd never expended so much time and energy on getting a woman into bed in his life. "Hey, how about a roll in the sack?" wouldn't exactly cut it.

So he decided to bring it out in the open. One afternoon they took a walk, with Tucker pushing the baby stroller and Maggie walking beside them. The weather was perfect, neither too hot or too cold, something that didn't occur often in this spot on the Texas coast.

One of the neighbors waved to them and
Maggie waved back. "Tucker, my arm is fine now.
I think you should go back to work tomorrow."

He glanced at her. "To tell you the truth, I've
enjoyed the break. But I do need to get back.
Janice has been phoning me daily with dire pre-
dictions of all my clients jumping ship if I don't
come back."

"There you go. Your secretary doesn't strike
me as the alarmist type."

Tucker laughed. "You don't know her very
well, then. It's par for the course for her." They
walked along in silence for a moment, then turned
back for the house. "Grace is nodding off," he
said. "We'd better go put her down for her nap."

"All right. I'll go to the store after we do. Otherwise we won't have anything for dinner."

"Why don't you wait on that? I want to talk
to you."

She shot him a suspicious glance, but didn't
protest. Once they'd put Grace down and left
her room they went to the den. He noticed she'd
grabbed her bag and was ready to head out the
door the instant they finished talking. He had
other plans.

"What do you want to talk about?" she asked
when he didn't speak.

"Have you seen the doctor about your arm?"

"I told you, it's fine now. But yes, Lana looked at it for me. She says it's fine, too."

"Good." He walked over to her and before she could give him any flak, put his arms around her and pulled her close. "Because I wanted to be sure you were all right before I did this again." He kissed her. Her lips had parted in surprise and he took full advantage, slipping his tongue in and enticing hers to answer. After stiffening initially, her body softened and she leaned into him.

For a brief moment, she answered in kind. Her arm came around his neck and she kissed him back, blasting his resolve to go slowly into a zillion pieces. He put his hands on her bottom and pressed her against him, deepening the kiss when he did so. He left her mouth and trailed his lips to the pulse beating rapidly at her throat. Wild images filled his mind of stripping her where she stood and taking her, on the floor, on the couch, against the wall. Anywhere, as long as he finally, *finally* had her.

"Tucker, stop."

He hesitated, trying to wrap his mind around her words. But he couldn't. So he moved to her jaw and tasted her there.

"Tucker, we have to stop."

She wanted him to stop? Now? He raised his head and looked at her then. "Why?"

She pushed at his chest and he reluctantly released her. It gave him little satisfaction to see her hand was unsteady when she reached up to brush her hair out of her face. "I—we—we can't do this. We can't make love."

"We nearly made love the other night," he reminded her. Maybe she could forget that, but he sure as hell couldn't. He'd never forget the sight of Maggie, lost in passion.

"I know." She closed her eyes briefly, then opened them. "And it would have been a mistake."

"That's a matter of opinion." He reached for her, making sure to take her uninjured arm because he knew the other was still tender. "Maggie, look at me and tell me you don't want me. Tell me you don't want to make love with me. Do it, and then I'll leave you alone."

She looked at him with tormented eyes. "I can't. You know I can't."

"Then what's stopping you?"

"It's just sex, Tucker. Hormones." She paced away and waved a hand. "We've been living together and we find each other attractive and neither of us has had sex in months now. It's just convenience, that's all it is. Our marriage is temporary and if we give in to this…urge, it will just make divorcing that much harder in the end."

Did she really believe what she was saying? "What if that's not all it is?"

She stared at him. "What do you mean?"

"What if what we have between us is more than sex? For both of us."

"It's not. It can't be."

"You sound very sure of that." He studied her a minute. "Tell me something, Maggie. What exactly is it about the two of us making love that scares you so much? Because you don't trust me…or because you don't trust anyone?"

"You don't understand." She twisted her hands together, gnawed on her lip before she squared her shoulders and faced him. "I don't *want* to want you. And I can't afford to trust you. Not about this."

His mind blank, he stared at her. He felt as if he'd been punched in the gut. And then her cell phone rang. "Goddamn it," he snarled. "Isn't that just typical."

She didn't bother to say she was sorry. She checked the number, then flipped open the phone. "This is Maggie. What's up, Chief?"

Tucker watched her face turn ashen as she listened. Devastated. He'd heard the word, used the word, but this was the first time he'd *seen* what it looked like.

"Here? In Aransas City? How do you know—" She listened impatiently, then said, "You're positive it's her? She has proof?" She gestured with her hand as if to cut him off. "I don't see how you can trust anything she says. You didn't tell her anything, did you? No, never mind, I know you didn't. I'll be right down. I want to question her myself." She didn't wait for an argument, just slapped the phone closed and looked at Tucker with pure terror in her eyes.

"What did he say?" Tucker asked, though he hardly needed to. Even what little he'd overheard didn't give it away as much as Maggie's demeanor. What she'd feared the most had finally happened.

Maggie passed a hand over her eyes and took in a deep breath. "Grace's mother— Carol Davis is down at the station right now. She just walked in, off the street, about half an hour ago."

"Are they sure it's Grace's mother?"

"They're sure. She had proof of her identity,

and of Grace's." Eyes anguished, she looked at him. "Tucker, she wants Grace back. She said she gave up her baby to protect her, and now the threat is gone and she wants her back."

CHAPTER SEVENTEEN

THE CHIEF STOPPED her at the door to the station house. "You just turn right around and go on home, Officer. Ralston is handling this case and you've got no call to be here."

"No call?" Maggie stared at him in disbelief. "I'm the child's foster mother."

"Which is exactly why this isn't your case. You can't be objective."

She bit off the hot words that bubbled on her tongue. She had to prove to the chief she could be professional. Calm, cool. Because she had every intention of seeing Grace's mother and questioning the woman herself. There was no way she'd trust that job to Ralston. He was a decent enough cop, but he wasn't very experienced, and certainly not in a case like this.

"Chief Corbitt, could we discuss this matter in your office?"

He eyed her for a moment, then jerked his

head toward his office and turned around. Maggie followed him, formulating how she was going to convince him to let her question the woman. *Grace's mother.* God, the thought itself had her in a panic.

Chief Corbitt took a seat, steepled his fingers on the desk in front of him and said, "Go ahead."

"I know this case better than anyone else, and certainly better than Ralston. She won't know that I'm anything more to Grace than the cop who found her. You know me, Chief. You know I'm a professional."

"Normally, yes. But this is different. Maggie, you're crazy about that baby. That makes you just about the worst person to be involved."

"No, it makes me the best. Please, just let me question her. You can sit in and if I step over the line you can cut me loose."

He pondered that, then sighed. "All right. You'll just badger me until I give in. But mind you keep it professional and don't let your feelings get in the way. Any tiny sign I see that you're going to lose it and you're out of there."

"Yes, sir."

A short time later Maggie and the chief walked into one of the conference rooms. A thin, pale, young blond woman, about eighteen or nineteen, sat at the battered table dressed in threadbare jeans and a T-shirt. She looked down on her luck, but her clothes had obviously been washed recently and her hair was clean, so she'd made an effort to look decent when she came in. And while the way she twisted her hands together suggested nerves, she didn't show any telltale signs of drug use. Not at first glance, anyway.

Okay, so Carol Davis might not be a junkie. She'd still abandoned her infant, which didn't exactly make her an upstanding citizen. And since the child in question was not a newborn, the safe haven law didn't apply.

"Carol Davis?"

"Yes." She looked at Maggie and then her eyes lit. "You're the officer who found my baby. How is she? No one will tell me anything. Is my baby all right?"

"I'm the officer who found an abandoned infant beside my patrol car, yes. We haven't established that you are, in fact, the mother of that infant."

"Please." She reached out and touched Maggie's arm. "Is Grace well? Is she all right?"

"The baby is fine. She's with Child Protective Services." *And me,* Maggie thought. At least for the present. "We'll assume for now you are the mother of the infant I found. Are you willing to explain why you abandoned your child?"

"I'll do whatever it takes to get Grace back. You—you hate me," she said, faltering. "I can see it in your eyes. You can't understand how I could leave my baby the way I did. How I could abandon her. I don't blame you. But I swear, I did it for Grace. To keep her safe."

"Do you understand that you could be charged with abandonment and possibly child endangerment as well? Those are very serious charges, Ms. Davis. Felonies."

She paled even more but she made an effort to hold herself together. "I understand. I know it was wrong, but I was desperate and I didn't know what else to do. I couldn't protect her any other way."

Maggie felt a pang of sympathy, but she hardened her heart. Carol Davis hadn't proved yet that she deserved any sympathy for abandoning her child. "You dumped your child like so much garbage, Ms. Davis. You left her sitting out in the open in the middle of February in a parking lot, for anyone to take. That could hardly be called protecting her."

"No! I saw the patrol car and I thought the

police could protect her. I thought they'd take her to CPS and find someone to care for her. And then I saw you go inside the building, so I—I put her beside your car for you to find when you returned. I hid in the bushes. I stayed right there and watched until you came back."

Maggie glanced at the chief, who hadn't said a word. "Why don't you tell us your story, Ms. Davis?" he said. "Start at the beginning and take it slowly."

Maggie sat down and opened her pad. She had a sick feeling in her gut that the woman's story was going to make her sound extremely sympathetic. And if that happened, Maggie stood no chance of retaining custody. If at all possible, CPS would side with the natural mother. As long as the child hadn't been abused…and Maggie knew full well that she hadn't.

"Grace's father left me when he found out I was pregnant. My parents had long since kicked me out. They didn't like Gerald and to be honest, they were just as glad to have an excuse to get rid of me. The morning sickness—" She shrugged and continued, "After I lost my job the only work I could find was at a bar in Corpus. A lot of bangers went there. It was bad, but I couldn't afford to be picky. Anyway, that's where I met Armand. He was nice. He tipped me and wouldn't let any of the others hassle me. At first, I just thought he was being nice. At first."

"This bar have a name? The gang have a name?"

She shook her head. "It's not important." She gave Maggie a sharp glance. "Besides, you know what happens to people who rat on bangers."

Yeah, she knew. "Go on."

"About six weeks after the baby was born, I was evicted. I found out later Armand had pressured the landlord to do it. He asked me to move in with him and I didn't have anywhere else to go, so I did." She halted, looked at Maggie and asked, "Could I have some water?"

The room doubled as a snack room, so Maggie got up, pulled a bottle out of the refrigerator and gave it to her before returning to her seat. She watched while Carol drank, then set the bottle down.

"Thank you." She drew in a breath and began again. "If I'd known what he would be like I would have chosen the streets. He didn't like the baby. He got angry every time Grace cried. He started talking about how he didn't want no 'other man's brat' around. I told him I'd leave.

That's the first time he hit me. He told me I was never leaving him. If anyone left it would be 'that goddamn squalling brat.'" Her voice broke and she looked at Maggie with loathing in her eyes. "That's what he called my precious baby. I knew what I had to do. It took me two weeks to plan how to get away. During that time I did everything he wanted me to. I let him use me, I let him hit me, I let him do whatever he wanted as long as he didn't hurt my baby. I prayed every day that Grace and I would get away. And finally, we did. I stole money for bus fare, took Grace and went to a friend, here in Aransas City. I guess I was stupid, because I didn't think Armand would bother to track me down."

Maggie could see it. All her words rang true. Carol Davis wasn't the monster of selfishness Maggie had imagined. She was an abused woman fleeing her abuser. Desperately afraid for her child. "What happened when he found you?"

"He said I was coming with him and that he was going to take care of my brat once and for all. He said he was going to kill her," Carol said stonily. "And he would have. I begged him to let me leave her with my friend, but he wouldn't hear of it. He—he wanted to kill her. To punish me." She stopped, drank more water, inhaled deeply and continued. "Angela wasn't home when he got there. She worked the late shift, so it was just Armand, me…and Grace. He said if Angela interfered, he'd kill her, too. And nobody could touch him, he said, because of his boys. He got really drunk and—" She halted, looking down at her hands clasped in front of her. "He raped me," she said flatly. "When he was finished, he passed out. I took Grace and walked out the door. That's when I saw the police car. So I left Grace there, and waited for you to come out. Once you did, I went back to the apartment and waited for him to wake up."

"Why didn't you wait for me and tell me what had happened? I would have helped you."

"He said he'd told his brothers where he was. If he didn't come back, they'd come find me and Grace and kill us. And Angela, too."

"You believed him," the chief said.

"Of course." Her voice was dull, unsurprised. "Killing us would be nothing to them. Killing, that's their life." She was silent, then said fiercely, "I wished I could be like them. I wanted to kill Armand. To just make him disappear. He was lying there, passed out and stinking drunk. I could have done it. But I was afraid. Afraid of what they'd do to Grace, to

Angela. To me. So I left Grace by your patrol car. And I went back with Armand. I told him I left Grace with a neighbor because if he killed her he'd get in trouble. He didn't care by then, he was just glad she was gone. Besides, he knew he had me to torture."

The chief didn't speak. He got up and left. And Maggie knew she'd already lost Grace.

"How did you get away this time? Aren't you afraid he'll come after you again?"

"He's dead. He died in a gang fight. The minute I heard the news, the minute I knew it was true, I left and came here for my baby." She touched Maggie's arm again. "Are you going to arrest me?"

"No." Even if Maggie had been inclined to, there wasn't a prosecutor in the world who'd take that case. Carol had been desperate, and she'd saved her child in the only way she knew. No one would condemn her for that, even if she hadn't chosen the best way to do it.

"And Grace?" she said quietly. "Will I get to keep Grace?"

"I don't know," she said, amazed she could sound so calm when her heart had been torn in two. "That's up to CPS."

Carol was openly crying now. "Do you think

they'll give her back to me? I love her so much. It's been killing me, not knowing what happened to her."

"You'll have to prove you're a fit parent. That you can take care of her and that you won't put her in danger again. You'll have to prove to them you won't be in a gang situation again." And she was going to have to prove it all to Maggie, as well, though she didn't know that yet.

Carol wiped her sleeve across her eyes. "I won't. I swear I won't. Angela said I could stay with her. She needs someone to share the rent. She has some leads on a job, too."

"I'll go call CPS and see if they can send someone over as soon as possible. I don't know what they'll say, but I recommend you be honest with them. Be sure and let them know you're looking for work and out of your previous situation. And you'd better mean it, because they won't just take your word for it. And neither will I."

"I do mean it. Thank you for your help, Officer—" She stopped and laughed. "I don't even know your name and you've been so kind."

"Officer Barnes," Maggie said. She'd never changed her name at work, knowing the marriage wouldn't last. But now it looked like it was going to be over sooner than even she had expected.

"Officer Barnes, thank you. And thank you for taking care of my little girl when you found her."

Maggie couldn't speak, so she nodded and left. Before she broke down completely.

CHAPTER EIGHTEEN

AN HOUR LATER, Maggie returned. Tucker took one look at her face—set, implacable, absolutely emotionless—and knew the news was really bad.

She laid her Glock on the table, then stripped off her equipment belt and laid that beside the gun, then started to leave the room. That alone told Tucker how upset she was. She hadn't left her weapon out since before they'd brought Grace home.

"Where's Grace?" she asked.

"She's asleep. Was it her mother?"

Maggie nodded. "Yes. I'm going to look in on Grace and then go work out."

Like hell she was. "Maggie, talk to me. Tell me what's going on. Are you charging the woman?"

"No." She didn't add anything else, just stood there looking blank.

"Why not?"

"Because she was an abused woman who protected her baby in the only way she knew how." She turned away from the hall and walked over to the window.

"By leaving her in a parking lot? Some protection."

Maggie turned back around. "It was the best she could do, given the circumstances."

Briefly, she told him the story Grace's mother had told her.

"So you're not going to do anything? You're just going to let this woman have Grace back as if she never did anything wrong? As if she never walked away from her without a backward glance?"

"CPS will handle it, but if she can prove she can provide a safe environment for Grace and take care of her properly, then yes, she'll get her back."

He simply stared at her. Maggie's mask slipped and he saw despair in her eyes. "No one would take the case, Tucker, if we did charge her. I saw her. Hell, I interrogated her. She was telling the truth. She was a victim and we can't condemn her for that. As for leaving Grace alone, she didn't. She hid nearby and watched me. She didn't leave until she knew Grace was in my custody."

"She could have just told you she waited. How do you know it's true?"

"She recognized me when I walked in the room."

"None of that makes what she did right. Why did she get involved with a gang member in the first place?" He went over to where Maggie stood, wanting to shake her out of her unnatural calm. No, he didn't want to shake her, he wanted to console her. Not that she'd allow it.

"She's young. Only eighteen. She was trying to survive. She met the banger at work and thought he was nice. He got her evicted from her apartment. She didn't know it was him, of course, so when he asked her to move in with him, she did. She had nowhere else to go."

He wanted to take Maggie in his arms, comfort her. But she radiated don't-touch signals. Afraid she'd break, he suspected. He remembered she'd said that after her miscarriage she'd sucked it up and gone on. That's what she was doing now. Alone. How could he make her understand she didn't have to do everything alone now?

Tucker put his hand on her arm and squeezed gently. "We could fight her. We could fight for custody of Grace."

"No. You didn't see her. She was a victim. I

can't victimize her again, and that's what we'd be doing if we fought for Grace." She paused and added, "She loves Grace. It must have killed her to give her up."

"You love Grace, too."

"I'm not Grace's mother. I never was. And now I never will be."

"Maggie—" He started to put his arms around her, but she held up a hand.

"Don't, Tucker. I appreciate the thought, but just…don't be nice. Don't be…anything. I have to— I'm going to box," she said abruptly and left the room.

She hadn't said, "And leave me the hell alone," but that's clearly what she meant. She didn't want him, his comfort, his advice, nothing. She didn't want *him*. And it was too damn bad that he wanted her more than he'd ever wanted anyone in his life. Because he wasn't going to get her. Ever.

LATER THAT EVENING Maggie was giving Grace a bottle when Tucker brought her the phone, looking grim-faced. She'd heard it ring but hadn't answered. She couldn't think of a soul she wanted to talk to. All she wanted was to spend time with Grace, though that was a double-edged sword, since every time she looked at the baby she wondered how much longer she'd be able to keep her.

"Who is it?" she said, not taking it.

"Nina Baker," he said. "From CPS."

He held out his arms and she put Grace into them and took the phone from him. She got up and walked out of the room, leaving Tucker the rocking chair. The fact that her friend had called Maggie herself instead of letting someone else in CPS do it was undoubtedly bad news and she didn't want to be around Grace when she heard it.

"It's Maggie."

"Maggie, it's Nina. How are you?"

She saw no reason to lie. "Not so great. What have you heard?"

"We've talked to Chief Corbitt and he says the police are not bringing charges. I talked to Grace's mother myself and I'm going to recommend she be allowed to retain custody of Grace once she has employment and a place to live. I wanted to tell you myself. I'm so sorry, Maggie. I know how attached you are to the baby."

Maggie doubted that, but she didn't say anything. It was what she'd expected, after all. Nina knew she cared about Grace but she had no idea the full extent of Maggie's "attach-ment" to the baby.

Nina continued, "Would it be possible for you to bring Grace to the CPS office tomorrow so her mother can see her? I'd like the first visit to be on neutral ground, and with her CPS case-worker present."

"Of course. What time?" Maggie marveled that she could sound so calm when she wanted to scream and rage. But that wouldn't do any good, so she clamped down on her emotions and did her best not to feel anything. The only thing she did feel was…frozen. Everything inside her had frozen the moment she'd heard Carol Davis's story, and she hadn't thawed out yet. Maybe she never would.

They settled on ten the next morning. Maggie went back to Grace's room, halting at the door to watch Tucker with Grace. They were so sweet together. She could imagine Tucker with a child of his own. He'd be a good father. A wonderful father. She entertained a brief, des-perate fantasy of herself with Tucker's child. Their child.

God, she was hopeless. He wanted to have sex with her. That didn't mean he wanted the same fantasy she did. Far from it. He'd married her as a favor, and now the favor was about to be unnecessary. Over and done with. If she wasn't selfish, she'd tell Tucker to start divorce proceedings right now. But she didn't. She couldn't face being alone, not yet. It wasn't fair to him, but she needed his support. The divorce would come soon enough, just as Grace would be gone soon. And Maggie would be alone, just as she'd always been.

"What did she want?" Tucker asked. He'd put the baby in her pajamas and now cuddled her against his shoulder as he patted her back.

"I'm taking Grace to see her mother in the morning. They want the first meeting to be at the CPS office."

"I'll go with you."

"You don't need to do that. I can take her myself."

"I know you can, but you're not going to. I'm coming with you."

She studied him a moment, then shrugged. She knew that when he had that face on he was unshakable. "We need to be there at ten."

The meeting with Carol the next day was every bit as hard as Maggie had feared it would be. Carol cried when she saw Grace, weeping unrestrainedly when she held the baby in her arms. Grace looked like her mother, Maggie realized, gazing at the two of them. And Carol Davis obviously loved her child. Emotion like she'd shown couldn't be faked.

After a while Carol calmed down and when she realized Maggie had been keeping Grace, she asked her a million questions about the baby's progress and all the things she'd missed over the past few months.

Tucker didn't say much but Maggie felt his presence and his support and was grateful for it. Because she knew that soon, not only would Grace no longer be in her life, but neither would Tucker.

Maggie was quiet on the way home, thinking about the visit. Carol had cried again when she'd had to leave Grace, but then she'd straightened her shoulders and wiped away the tears. "I'll have a job by the end of the week," she'd told the caseworker. When the woman had asked her what she'd be doing Carol had replied, "Whatever it takes. I want my child back and I'm not afraid to work to make that happen."

Maggie wanted to hate Carol for taking Grace away from her, but she couldn't. Everything she'd told Tucker was true. And she admired Carol for facing the situation and trying her best to overcome it. She resolved to talk to Delilah and see if she and Cam had an opening of any sort at their restaurant. She also had the number of a woman who did child care in her home and had flexible hours. Maggie had thought about using her when she went back to work. Now she'd give the number to Carol Davis.

At least if Carol stayed in Aransas City, Maggie would be able to see Grace occasionally. Although she wasn't sure that wouldn't be worse than not seeing her at all. But she wanted to make certain that Grace was happy and cared for. Grace was the important one in this situation. What did Maggie's feelings matter as long as the baby was safe and happy and loved?

"You're awfully quiet," Tucker said, breaking in to her thoughts.

"I'm just tired. I haven't slept very well lately." Not since she got the news about Grace's mother.

"I know. I've heard you up during the night." He picked up her hand and squeezed it. "I watched you with her. With Grace's mother. You're amazing."

Surprised, she looked at him. "Why?"

"Because you're doing what you think is best for Grace and her mother, no matter what it costs you."

"She's barely more than a kid herself, Tucker. Carol Davis has been kicked just about every way there is, and she's still fighting. She's fighting to be with her baby. I'm going to help her do that."

"Even though it kills you," he said quietly.

"Even then."

CHAPTER NINETEEN

THE DAY MAGGIE had dreaded finally dawned. It should have been dark and dreary to match her mood, but it was a beautiful day, crystal clear, mid-eighties, with a light breeze blowing and less humidity than usual. She tried once again to talk Tucker into going to work.

"I'm not going to fall apart, you know. You can go on to work. I'll be fine." And she would. She was blessedly numb. She only hoped she stayed that way long enough to hand Grace over to her mother. "Besides, I'm going to work as soon as Carol leaves." She didn't know if working would keep her mind off the baby, but at least it would give her something to do besides stare at the walls and miss Grace.

Tucker was sitting at the kitchen table, watching her give Grace a bottle. "I can go in later. Has it occurred to you that I'm going to miss Grace, too?"

It hadn't, really. She felt like a jerk. "I know you care about her, I just—"

"I love her, too, Maggie," he said flatly. "You can't be around a baby like Grace for as long as we have and not fall for her."

Now she felt like an even bigger jerk. "I'm sorry, Tucker. I'm sorry I dragged you into this and now you're hurting, too." She got up and put Grace in his arms, to let him finish feeding her. "I'm going to get the rest of her things ready."

Tucker came in with Grace a little while later. "Are you sure you know what you're doing giving her all the baby's furniture and toys?"

"I might as well. All Carol has is a crib and most of this stuff will be really useful for her. Besides, I'm not going to be using any of it."

"Ever?"

Her heart twisted but she said calmly enough, "I would want a husband to have a child and I won't have one for very much longer."

"It doesn't have to be that way."

Shocked, she turned to look at him. Surely he didn't mean that like it had sounded. "What do you mean?"

"We don't have to get divorced."

Her stomach rolled. If he was trying to make her feel better it sure as hell wasn't working.

Because she realized she wanted more than anything to stay married to Tucker. To have a real marriage with him. But Tucker didn't want that. He'd only said it to comfort her. She'd already conned him into a marriage he hadn't wanted; the least she could do was stay true to her word and give him a divorce.

"Divorce was the plan," she said lightly. "I don't see any reason to change it."

He didn't say anything, just gazed at her for a long moment before turning away and putting Grace down on the changing table. "What do you want her to wear?" he asked, and the moment passed.

Ten minutes later the doorbell rang. Her eyes met Tucker's. Wordlessly, he gave her Grace and went to answer the door.

"I love you," Maggie whispered to the baby and kissed her cheeks, then her soft, fine hair. Grace smiled and waved a chubby fist in the air.

Maggie walked out of the bedroom and put Grace into her mother's arms, then helped Tucker and Carol's friend load everything into the truck.

"I don't know how to thank you," Carol said when they finished. "Not just for this—" she gestured to the loaded truck "—but for everything you did for Grace, and for taking such good care of her. Will you come see us?"

Maggie nodded. Although she knew CPS was on the case, she'd check on them to make sure everything was all right, as well.

Maggie watched the truck drive away, standing there staring after it until they were long gone. Tucker came over and put his arm around her and watched with her.

"Come on," he said gruffly. "Let's go inside."

She let him lead her. She felt...nothing. Empty. Tucker still hadn't let go of her, she realized. He must think she was going to break down, but that was the last thing she intended to do. She moved away from him. "I'm going in to work. I should be back around dinner."

"Don't go in, Maggie. Stay here with me."

"No." Her throat closed up and she felt herself losing it. "I need to work, Tucker. It will take my mind off...everything." Work had been her solace in the past. It would be again.

He walked over to her and took her limp hands in his. "Do what you need to do. But I want you to know, I'm here for you."

God, she wished she could accept his offer of comfort. Wished she could allow herself to depend on him, on his strength, on his caring.

But she couldn't. She'd already committed the ultimate folly of falling in love with him. Depending on him now would only make it that much harder when he left. Because Tucker was going to leave her, just as Grace had. Just as her parents had. Just as everyone she loved left her.

TUCKER PICKED UP a pizza for dinner, even though he wasn't hungry and he doubted Maggie would be. But he meant to see that she ate something, regardless. He knew that taking care of herself was the last thing on her mind, so he'd try to do it for her. He hadn't been surprised that she'd gone to work immediately. That's how Maggie coped with what life threw at her. By sucking it up and going on.

Her lack of emotion wasn't natural, though, and he believed it was only a matter of time until she broke down. He'd meant what he'd told her that morning. He intended to be there for her, whether she wanted him to be or not.

He wouldn't think about how much he, too, missed Grace. Maggie was the important one here.

Her patrol car was in the driveway and her personal car in the garage, so he knew she was home. He threw the pizza box down on the kitchen table and went in search of her. He could not only hear it, but he felt the vibrations of the music coming from the exercise room. Expecting to find Maggie beating the hell out of the punching bag, he opened the door and stepped inside. She wasn't by the bag.

He scanned the room and found her huddled in the corner with her knees drawn up to her chest. Crying. No, weeping. Passing by the boom box, he clicked it off, and in three quick strides he was beside her. "It's about time," he said. He sat down and pulled her into his lap, put her head on his shoulder and his arms around her. "Damn it, Maggie. I'm so sorry."

It said volumes that she didn't bother to fight him. She simply turned her body into his and continued to cry. It hurt him to hear her so desolate and not be able to help, but he thought crying it out was likely the best thing for her—the only thing that might make her feel even a little better. So he held her, comforted her, murmured soothing words into her hair as she sobbed.

She held something clenched in her hand. Something pink. One of Grace's socks, he realized. He felt a lump in his own throat, seeing the tiny reminder of the baby they would both miss so much.

A long time later, she finally ran down. Tucker still held her, not at all anxious to let her go. He picked up the towel lying beside them and wiped her tears, then gave it to her to blow her nose. Wordlessly, he took the sock in exchange for the towel and put it in his pocket, out of her sight.

"Better?"

"Not really. More like empty," she said, her voice hoarse with tears.

He tucked her hair back behind her ear, then, intending only comfort, he kissed her. For a moment she was perfectly still, then her arms went around his neck in a stranglehold and she kissed him back. He tasted salt from her tears. And heat, a river of it, flowing out of her.

She pulled back and locked eyes with him, hers still tormented. "Make love to me, Tucker."

Oh, God, he wanted to. But not like this, not with her so sad, so despairing. "Maggie—"

She interrupted him by kissing him. When he would have spoken she kissed him again, her tongue sweeping his mouth with desperate urgency. "Make me forget. Make me feel something, anything besides this pain that won't stop."

He was only a man, not a saint. And she was soft, yielding, reckless in his arms. He loved her and he wanted her so much. Had wanted her forever, it seemed to him.

He pushed her shirt up, cupped her bare breasts. Rubbed his palms over her nipples as they stiffened into taut peaks. Maggie reached for the hem of her shirt, tugged it off and tossed it aside. Her fingers reached for his shirt, swearing as she fumbled to unbutton it.

His mouth came down on hers, hard. Kissing her, consuming her, wanting all of her, as quickly as he could have her. Impatient with her progress, he jerked his shirt over his head and lay down with her, between her thighs. He kissed her mouth, then left it to suckle her breasts. Her hands were in his hair, urging him on, her hips bucking against his.

She moaned. "Tucker," she said on a sob.

He stripped off her shorts and panties, got rid of his own pants and came back to her open arms, lying between her silky thighs, pushing at the entrance to her body. She was wet, wild and shuddering and he sank inside her in one desperate push.

"Hurry," she said, her nails scoring his back.

He knew it was too soon for her, but he couldn't hold back and she clearly didn't want him to. Her body gloved him, stroked him with her muscles clenching as he drove into her and pulled back, again and again until he exploded inside her, in endless spasms.

Her eyes were heavy, slumberous, her lips puffy from his kisses, her hair messed up from his hands. She looked more beautiful than he'd ever seen her, even though she wore her sadness like another layer of skin. "More," he said, kissing her lips.

She kissed him, her tongue sliding against his and whispered, "More."

He carried her into his bedroom, lay her on his bed and followed her down. This time he took her slowly, seduced her until she writhed and quivered for him, and she climaxed screaming his name.

They drifted to sleep in each other's arms and he knew he'd do anything to keep her here, like this, in his bed, in his life, in his heart.

CHAPTER TWENTY

EARLY THE NEXT MORNING Maggie woke in Tucker's bed, but he wasn't beside her. As she lay there, the night before came back to her in a collage of images. She and Tucker making love through the night, until they both fell into an exhausted sleep. Waking, eating cold pizza in bed, then making love again. He couldn't get enough of her, and she felt the same, tracing her hands over his lean, muscular body, letting him take her places she'd only dreamed about.

Nothing she'd ever experienced had compared to what they'd shared the night before. No one, not even Spencer, had made her feel what Tucker did. She loved him. Completely, totally. And she had to let him go.

Maybe it wasn't real, but it had felt real enough when he was loving her.

The night was a blur of lovemaking and she knew she would be sore. That would go away, though. There was one thing that might not. They hadn't used birth control. Not until they'd already made love twice.

After the second time, he'd asked her if she was taking anything. She'd said no, but told him it was the wrong time of month. Which it was…just barely. Tucker had taken some condoms out of his drawer and she'd seduced him again and neither of them thought about anything for a very long time.

One night. Just a couple of times. *It only takes once,* she thought, remembering her previous pregnancy. But no good would come of worrying. She'd put it out of her mind and pray nothing had happened.

The night before, when she was hurting so much, there had been some excuse for her lack of caution. But she'd been behaving irresponsibly from day one, when she cooked up the scheme to marry Tucker so she could keep Grace. She found it hard to forgive herself for any of her actions.

Tucker walked in and gave her a mug of coffee. "Thanks." Feeling self-conscious, she pulled the sheet over her breasts before she sat up and sipped the hot brew. "God, I love the first cup of coffee in the morning."

He smiled and sat down on the bed next to her. He wore a pair of jeans and nothing else. She couldn't help looking at his bare chest and remembering the feel of it beneath her hands. Remembering trailing kisses across his chest and down his abdomen….

"I know exactly how you feel," he said. "Are you going to work today?"

"Not until eleven, and I get off at four. The chief has me on limited duty." She took another sip and frowned. "I think he's afraid I'm going to lose it."

"I doubt it. He's just trying to give you a break."

His hand caressed her arm. She wished that simply seeing him, much less having him touch her, didn't make her want him again. She had to call a halt to this newfound intimacy. "Do you want to file or should I?"

His hand still stroked her skin, making her shiver. "File what?" he asked absently.

"File for divorce."

His hand stopped its movement and he stared at her, a frown gathering. "Are you trying to piss me off?"

"No, I'm trying to be practical. The reason for our marriage no longer exists. Grace is with her mother now."

"You can ask me for a divorce after last night? After we made love—hell, I can't even count how many times? Are you kidding me?"

"Last night was about comfort, for both of us. You and I both know that."

"That's all you think it was? Comfort?"

He had dropped his hand but he still sat beside her. Too close. "I know that's all it was. So, who's filing for the divorce?"

"Neither of us."

"Tucker—"

He held up a hand to stop her. "There's no reason to rush into a divorce. I'm hurting, Maggie. Maybe not as much as you are, but I have feelings. I told you yesterday, I love Grace, too. Why make losing her any harder on us than it already is? Besides, you don't even have a place to stay."

True. Her house was rented for another several months. But there was no way she could stay with Tucker for too long. Not that it mattered. The damage was already done. She'd been in love with him for weeks now.

"All right, we can wait a little longer. But I don't think we should have sex again."

For a minute he simply stared at her and then a sly smile curved his mouth. "You don't think we should make love again," he repeated.

His dark hair was messed up, probably from her running her fingers through it a hundred times. The stubble on his face gave him a sexy, almost rakish air. Coupled with that devilish expression in those gorgeous blue eyes, she didn't trust him, not one tiny inch.

"That's right. I don't."

He reached for her mug and placed it on the bedside table. Then he stepped back and calmly stripped out of his blue jeans.

"Tucker! What are you doing?"

In about twenty seconds he stood in front of her, stark naked and very aroused. And smiling that same devilish smile. Maggie knew she was toast. Still, she tried.

"Put your clothes back on. This is crazy! We're not going to—"

He stopped her argument by leaning down and kissing her. Her body betrayed her. She wanted him, and he knew it, damn it. He got into bed with her, pulled down the sheet and stroked her breasts slowly. They had already tightened in anticipation, and she felt herself growing damp instantly, aching with need. "Damn you, Tucker," she murmured against his mouth.

"You might as well face it." His hand slid between her legs and he cupped her, exploring her boldly as he strung kisses along her jaw. "This particular Pandora's box has been well and truly opened. And it's not going to close anytime soon."

She pushed him onto his back, reached for a condom and sheathed him with it. Then she straddled him, teasing him with her body until they were both wild with need. "I hate when you're right," she said, and took him inside her. Seconds later, she came in a torrent of pleasure, then felt Tucker spend himself inside her with her name on his lips.

She couldn't move so she lay on top of him, boneless and exhausted. Tucker was right. Celibacy was out of the question now. She might as well enjoy him for as long as they had together.

Even if they couldn't spend every moment in bed together, at least there would be long periods of time when she wouldn't have to think about the mess she'd made of her life. And what she intended to do about it.

HE'D AVOIDED THE AX, Tucker thought a couple of weeks later, but each day was a new battle. Maggie still seemed determined to go through with the divorce. Even though he talked her out of it every time she mentioned filing, which was damn near daily, he felt pretty powerless to stop it ultimately.

You can't make someone love you, she'd once said. And he was trying everything he knew how to make her fall for him and so far, he'd failed spectacularly. It appeared Maggie was right on about that.

"Tucker, are you all right?"

He glanced up at his secretary. How long had she been standing in front of him? "I'm fine. What did you need, Janice?"

Janice was in her mid-fifties and scarily efficient. She tapped the pad she held in her hands with a pen. "You called me in to discuss the Atkins file with me. But you've been out in the ozone for the past five minutes since I've been standing here."

"Sorry, my mind was elsewhere." On his wife. His soon-to-be ex-wife unless he figured out a way to convince her to drop that idea. "Can you get my father on the phone? We can take care of that business later. It will keep."

"Of course, I'll be glad to." She shot him a considering glance as she left.

He massaged his temples and wished he could concentrate on his work, but that obviously wasn't happening. It pissed him off, because he never neglected work and he didn't intend to start now. Even though he didn't have anything pressing currently, he still had clients and they still had needs. Now, if Maggie would just relax and let him— He wadded up the piece of paper he'd been making notes on and threw it across the room. Damn it, he was doing it again.

He arranged to meet his father for lunch at the Scarlet Parrot. He walked in at noon to find his father there before him. Delilah Randolph greeted him as he came in. They chatted briefly, then she put her hand on his arm. "I don't want to bring up painful subjects, but I was so sorry to hear about Grace. Not that I'm not happy for her mother, but I know how hard giving her up must be on you and Maggie."

"Thanks. It's worse for Maggie."

"I saw you with the baby, Tucker. It's hard on you, too. But at least you and Maggie have each other."

For now. And Maggie wasn't talking. Every night he tried to get her to talk about her feelings, but she refused. She'd let him make love to her, but she wouldn't talk. Not about anything important, and not one word about Grace. "Has she talked to you about Grace?"

Delilah shook her head. "Nothing beyond the

bare fact that Grace's mother had returned and Grace was going to live with her. But you know Maggie likes to keep things close."

Understatement of the decade. They reached the table where his father waited. Tucker shook his hand and ordered an iced tea.

They talked for a few minutes and after the waitress dropped off their drinks and took their orders, Harvey said, "Is there something particular you wanted to talk about?"

"Yeah. And I'd appreciate it if you didn't tell Mom." His mother would probably advise him to divorce Maggie and forget about her. However, she'd been surprisingly sympathetic when he'd told his parents about Grace, and had even asked if there was anything she could do for Maggie.

"Not if you don't want me to. What's wrong?"

Unsure how to begin, he took a sip of tea. "I'm in love with Maggie," he blurted out.

"I could point out that you're married and supposed to be in love with your wife, but I take it that's a problem," Harvey said after a moment.

"Oh, yeah. She's not in love with me. She only married me because of Grace." He told him the story then, about the bargain they'd struck, including the part about no sex.

Harvey laughed. "I find it hard to believe you agreed to that condition."

"So, I was stupid. I'd convinced myself all I felt for her was friendship. That didn't last long, for me, anyway. Then, the night Grace left… Maggie was hurting and looking for comfort." He paused, thinking about that night. It hadn't been all about comfort, regardless of what she said the morning after. "I didn't take advantage of her, if that's what you're thinking. I tried not to, but I—she—" He broke off, shrugging, not wanting to go into detail. "Anyway, it happened."

"I think you were hurting as much as Maggie was, Tucker. I know you love the baby. There's nothing wrong with turning to your wife for comfort."

"Even if she isn't really your wife?"

"The marriage may have started out a sham, but it sounds like the real thing now."

The waitress returned with their food and after eating a few bites, Tucker continued. "That's the problem. It's not a sham, not on my part. But now that Grace is with her mother, Maggie says the reason for the marriage no longer exists. She keeps bringing up divorce, and that's the last thing I want."

Harvey ate a bite, then asked, "Have you told her you don't want a divorce?"

"Not exactly. So far I've just been dragging my feet." And seducing her every night. He'd thought making love would strengthen their relationship, but even though Maggie clearly enjoyed the sex, Tucker knew she was holding part of herself back. He applied himself to his food without much interest.

"Let me take a wild guess. You haven't told her you're in love with her, either."

"No." He'd been picking at his food, but at that he glanced up at his father. "Do you think I should?"

Harvey blotted his lips with his napkin. "Frankly, Tucker, I can't figure out why you haven't already told her. How can you expect her to know what you feel when you haven't talked to her about anything?"

"I didn't want to know for a fact she isn't in love with me."

"That's a remarkably negative way of looking at it. And not like you at all."

Tucker pinched the bridge of his nose. "I haven't been myself since the day Maggie talked me into marrying her. She's making me crazy. Usually I'm good at reading people. But

Maggie takes keeping her cards close to her chest to a whole new level."

"Tell her how you feel, Tucker. You might be surprised to find out she's in love with you, too."

Maybe. But what would he do if she wasn't?

CHAPTER TWENTY-ONE

"MAGGIE, IT'S SO GOOD to see you," Lana said. "I can't tell you how many times I started to go next door and then realized you weren't there. Come on in." She opened the door wider and waved Maggie inside.

"Thanks. I hope you don't mind but I thought I'd catch you at home. I know you take off Wednesday afternoons."

"Since when have I ever minded you dropping by? Did you think that would change just because you got married?"

"No, but I didn't want to catch you in the middle of something."

"I'm not doing a thing." She patted her stomach, which was huge. "I'm supposed to be nesting. I'm due in a week and Gabe's been having a fit that I haven't quit work yet. He wants me to start maternity leave yesterday," she said with a laugh. "I just can't see sitting home waiting to deliver, though."

"Maybe it will happen sooner than you think."

Lana lowered herself carefully into the rocking chair. "I sure hope so. Gabe is driving me crazy hovering over me." She sighed and added, "He's even taken on more help at the shop so he can be with me more often now that my due date is so close. Which is great, don't get me wrong. But who knew he'd be such a mother hen?"

Maggie stifled a pang of envy. She didn't begrudge Gabe and Lana their happiness, she knew how much they deserved it. If only she hadn't made such a royal mess of her own life, she might have shared that same kind of happiness with someone. Not just someone, she thought. Tucker.

"Is Gabe here, then? I didn't see his truck out front. Don't tell me he cleaned out the garage enough to fit both cars in there."

"No, no," Lana said, laughing. "I thought since he has all this free time, he might as well be useful. I sent him to buy ice cream. He should be back any minute."

"I need to ask you something before Gabe comes back. And would you mind not saying anything to him? Or to anyone?"

Lana sat up straight and pinned her with a sharp glance. "Are you having a medical problem, Maggie? Why didn't you come to the clinic? Of course I wouldn't talk about your medical concerns."

"I didn't come to the clinic because I didn't want Tucker to hear about it. It would be just my luck that his secretary would see me go in or worse, his mother. I just need to ask you a question. How accurate are those early pregnancy tests you can buy?"

"Some are more accurate than others. How early are we talking? False negatives are fairly common if it's taken before you miss a period."

"My period is three days late and I'm normally regular as clockwork."

"They're about ninety-seven percent accurate at that point."

"What about false positives? Are they common, too?"

"No. False positives do occur, but they're rare. I could give you a blood test. They're extremely accurate. Do you think you're pregnant, Maggie?"

Maggie sat on the couch. Her head was reeling, even though she wasn't surprised. First off, she'd barely managed not to barf the last few mornings. After she took the test earlier that morning, she'd decided to check with Lana, just to make sure. If she was having a baby she wanted Lana to be her doctor. Unless… "Are you planning to go back to work after the baby is born?"

Lana smiled. "Yes. I'll take a couple of months off and then I'll go back part-time. So you do think you're pregnant."

She nodded. "The test I took this morning was positive. And I've been queasy in the mornings."

"I'd say you are most likely pregnant, then." Lana studied her a moment. "Forgive me, but you don't seem very happy about it."

"I am happy," Maggie said, fighting back tears. "But I'm miserable, too."

Lana leaned forward and grasped her hand. "Do you want to talk about it?"

Grateful for the support, Maggie shook her head. "I don't know. It's complicated." And how in the hell was she going to explain this whole debacle to anyone without sounding totally insane?

"Are you and Tucker having problems? You seem so happy together."

"It's hard to explain. Can I ask you something else? About pregnancy?"

"Of course."

"I had a miscarriage before. Does that mean I'm more likely to have one this time, too?"

"Not necessarily. It depends on the reason you miscarried."

"The doctor said it was just one of those things. It was early, in the first trimester."

"I can't say for sure without examining you, but again, I don't think you necessarily have to be concerned about another miscarriage."

Her anxiety eased up a bit. "Good."

"Does Tucker know you're pregnant?"

"No." And if she could possibly work it, he wasn't going to know until they were divorced. Or at the least, until after they filed.

They heard the back door slam and Gabe's voice came from the kitchen. "I bought four different kinds of ice cream. Well, three and a half," he said, coming into the room with a quart of ice cream in one hand and a spoon in the other. "I put the rest in the freezer."

Lana looked at her husband and said, "Gimme."

"Hey, Maggie. Long time no see," Gabe said. "There's a little matter of payment," he told his wife, leaning over and tapping a finger on his lips.

Lana laughed and kissed him. "Now, gimme."

He grinned at her and handed her the ice cream.

"I've got to get going," Maggie said. "Good to see both of you."

"Let me see you to the door," Lana said.

"No, don't get up," Maggie protested, but Lana ignored her. It took her a while to make it, but with Gabe's help she finally did and walked Maggie to the front door. "I mean it," she said in a low voice. "Anytime you want to talk you know I'm here. And whenever you're ready, make an appointment to see me so I can examine you. I'll tell our receptionist to get you in right away once you call."

"Thanks, Lana."

"Don't wait too long."

"I won't. I'll call soon." She definitely wanted Lana to be her doctor, but she doubted she'd take her up on the offer of talking. Lana was great, and she'd be understanding, Maggie was sure. But Lana was also about to have a baby with a husband who was crazy about her and their coming child. How pathetic would Maggie sound if she told Lana the story of her fake marriage? No, better to keep it to herself. Besides, there was only one course of action. She just hoped she was strong enough to follow it.

SHE MEANT TO TALK to Tucker as soon as he came home. Clean and quick and get it over with. But Tucker didn't give her the chance. He didn't so much as say hello when he came into the kitchen from the garage. Instead, he spun her around and kissed her to within an inch of her life. He tasted hot, potent. His hands fell to her hips and pulled her closer. Her breasts started tingling and her body went lax. She loved him so much. Didn't she deserve to be with him one last time? To make love with him?

No, she didn't deserve it. Not when she was about to lie to him. "Tucker, wait. We need to talk."

"Later." He reached beneath her shirt and cupped her breasts, then popped the front clasp on her bra and filled his hands with her bare breasts.

Maggie shivered at the feel of his palms on her bare skin. She should resist. But she didn't.

"I've been thinking about you all day," he said. "About making love to you." He kissed her again, thrusting his tongue deep inside her mouth, slow, wet and wild.

The next thing she knew he'd stripped her and boosted her onto the kitchen table. His mouth felt wonderful on her breasts. She should say something, anything, to stop him, but she didn't have the will. She loved him, she wanted to be with him, one last time.

He reached into his pocket and pulled out a condom. A condom he didn't need, but she didn't tell him that. Instead, she watched as he placed it on the table beside her, then put his mouth to her stomach.

"You are so beautiful," he murmured against the skin of her stomach. His lips trailed down, creating rivers of sensation, and then she felt the sweep of his tongue at her center.

"Tucker, wait," she said, putting her hands in his hair and pushing him away, even as her hips lifted to meet him.

His tongue slicked over her slowly, then he raised his head. "Why?"

She couldn't tell him that the last time he'd made love to her this way she'd barely maintained control. It had been too intense, too... shattering. And that had been deep in the night, in the darkness of their bedroom. How much more vulnerable was she now, in the light of day, naked with him still fully clothed? How much more vulnerable knowing that this was the last time they would make love?

"I want you inside me," she said. But she knew, no matter how they made love that she couldn't keep the distance between them. The only way to do that was to leave him.

Something flickered in his eyes. She couldn't tell if it was anger or hurt or something else entirely. He didn't say anything, but simply stood back and stripped, then sheathed himself and stepped between her legs.

She closed her eyes and waited.

"Maggie, look at me." His voice was rough and hoarse.

Though she knew it was a mistake, she opened her eyes. He lifted her hips and thrust into her with a smooth motion. She wrapped her legs around him, shuddering as he pushed into her and pulled out in a deep, driving rhythm. His eyes were shining and he kept them locked on hers as he made love to her.

Her body tightened. Her climax built, layer upon layer until it hovered just out of reach. Each time she thought she'd peak, he'd pull back, slow things down, then build her back up until she nearly screamed at the sweet torment.

His eyes still on hers, Tucker thrust deep inside her and she shattered, his name bursting from her in a sob of pleasure so intense she thought she'd died. Moments later, he followed her over, groaning her name as he spent himself inside her.

She didn't move. She couldn't. The most she

could manage was to hold him until their breathing slowed.

"Why is it so hard for you to let anyone get close to you?" Tucker asked her long minutes later with his head resting on her breast.

She wanted to cry. "We're naked and you're still inside me. How much closer do you want to be?"

He raised his head and looked at her. He looked more sad than anything else. "You know what I'm talking about, Maggie. You share your body but since that first night we made love, there's been a barrier. Every time we make love. You wouldn't have dropped that barrier this time if I hadn't pushed you into it."

Her heart was breaking into a thousand pieces. "Leave it alone, Tucker. Please, just… don't talk about it."

He didn't say anything else. Simply moved away from her, picked up his clothes and walked out of the room. Maggie's throat closed up and she fought back the tears. When she gained control, she dressed. Then she went to find Tucker and tell him their marriage was over.

CHAPTER TWENTY-TWO

TUCKER PICKED UP a heavier dumbbell and started another set. He'd rather be indulging in a nice, lazy postcoital glow, snuggling with his wife, but instead he was lifting weights, trying to get rid of the anger riding him.

He'd been primed to tell Maggie he loved her. And then he'd made love to her and sensed that damn distance she was always putting between them. She didn't want to be close to him. How many more times did she have to prove that to him before he believed it?

She enjoyed the sex. He knew that. But he wanted more. He wanted her to love him…and it was pretty damn clear she didn't.

"Tucker, we need to talk."

Glancing up, he saw Maggie in the doorway. She had her cop face on, which meant he couldn't read her at all. But he had a feeling he wasn't going to like what she wanted to talk about. He continued to lift, moving his forearm in a bicep curl. "So talk."

"Could you quit doing that?"

He finished the set, then put the dumbbell down and looked at her. She walked farther into the room but she didn't sit down. But then, the only place to sit was beside him on the weight bench.

"I'm going to file for divorce tomorrow."

Great. They made love and she decided to divorce him. "I thought we'd agreed to wait on that."

"We have waited. Grace has been with her mother for almost three weeks. It's time to do what we planned."

"Plans can change. I don't think we should get divorced right now." Or ever, but he couldn't seem to say that.

"The only reason I can think of to stay married would be if we were in love with each other. And we're not."

Not entirely accurate. One of them was. But why should he lay his heart on the line when she'd only crush it? "There's one other reason to stay married."

"I can't think of one."

"I can. Say, if you were pregnant."

She didn't say anything. Worse, she flushed

and looked away. *Oh my God.* Anger, and hurt, burned in his stomach. "You're pregnant."

"It doesn't matter if I'm pregnant or I'm not. I'm filing for divorce tomorrow."

He reached her before she could run out the door, halting her with his hand on her arm. "When were you going to tell me?" She didn't answer. "Goddamn it, Maggie. Answer me. You owe me that, at least. Were you going to tell me?"

She hesitated for a long moment, then she looked at him, misery in her expression. "Yes. After we were divorced."

He didn't trust himself to speak. She would have denied him his child. Not permanently; he knew her better than that. But long enough to make sure they divorced before he knew about it.

"We are not getting divorced when you're pregnant with my baby."

"This is exactly why I didn't want to tell you until after we filed. I knew you'd fight me if you knew I was pregnant."

"You're damn right I will." Oh, to hell with it. He wasn't going to hang on to his pride when she was about to destroy their lives. He pulled her closer. "The baby isn't the only reason I don't want a divorce." She looked suspicious, angry. Not in the best frame of mind to hear his confession. But he plowed on, determined to say it. "I'm in love with you, Maggie." Even though he didn't think she loved him. Even though she'd hurt him more than he would have believed. He still loved her.

Her expression changed to one of disbelief. "Are you? Or are you just saying that because I'm pregnant?"

"I mean it. I love you, and it has nothing to do with the baby."

"It's a little ironic that you didn't think to mention this fact until after you found out I was pregnant. Not once before this have you ever said you loved me."

He started to yell, but forced himself to be calm. "I was going to tell you today. When I came home. And then I saw you and we made love and—" To hell with being calm. "Damn it, Maggie, I didn't tell you because you were doing your 'let me put as much distance between Tucker and me as possible' routine."

She shook him off and moved away. "I'm not trapping you in a loveless marriage simply because I'm pregnant. It wouldn't be right."

"We don't have a loveless marriage! I'm in love with you!"

She shook her head. "Don't. Don't do this, Tucker. Just let me file and don't fight me."

This was spiraling out of control so fast he couldn't possibly save it. But he had to try. "Do you think I'd lie to you about something this important?"

"You're damn right I do. If the lie resulted in you being able to do what you believe is the right thing. But it's not, Tucker."

She didn't believe him. Wouldn't believe him, no matter what he said. Or worse, maybe she did believe him and wanted to let him down easy. "You're not in love with me. That's the answer, isn't it? That's why you refuse to believe I love you."

"My feelings aren't the issue," she said. "I'm going to file in the morning." She walked out and this time he let her go.

It hurt, more than he would have believed possible, to know Maggie didn't love him and apparently didn't think she ever could. Their marriage had always been about the baby, not about the two of them. First Grace and now their unborn child. Maggie was pregnant. Unlike when she'd wanted to keep Grace, this time she didn't need to live with a man she didn't love in order to have a child.

"TUCKER, WAKE UP."

"Hmm." He cracked open an eye and realized Maggie was standing beside his bed, shaking him. Every miserable scene from the night before came flooding back. He sat up. "What? What's wrong?"

"I think I'm losing the baby," she said, and burst into tears.

He reached for her. "Sit down. Come on, sit and tell me what happened."

She did as he said, wiping her eyes and trying to maintain control but she wasn't very successful.

"Take a deep breath," Tucker said, putting his arm around her and giving her a comforting hug. "And then tell me."

"I got up to go to the bathroom and I—I saw it. There was blood. I'm spotting."

He knew absolutely nothing about pregnancy. "I take it that's not normal."

"I don't know. All I know is last time…when I lost the baby, that's how it started. Bleeding, cramping, and then I lost it."

"We need to call your doctor. Is it Lana?" He figured she was, since the two of them were friends.

"Yes, Lana. But we can't call her now. It's

two-thirty in the morning. She's due in a week and she needs her sleep."

"I'm sure she won't mind." He started to get up but Maggie clutched his arm.

"I'm so scared," she whispered. "What if I lose this baby, too? What if—"

He put his fingers to her lips. "Don't, Maggie." He put his arm around her again and hugged her, kissed her cheek. "Talk to Lana. It could be nothing." He didn't know if that was true or not, but he knew what she needed to hear.

He found the cordless phone, and after Maggie gave him the number, punched it in. Lana answered on the second ring. "Lana, it's Tucker. I'm sorry to call you so late, but Maggie's having a problem. She really needs to talk to you." He handed Maggie the phone.

He didn't hear a lot, partly because Maggie was crying and partly because she didn't say much after she explained her symptoms. Finally, Maggie said, "Okay, I'll come in tomorrow at eight-thirty," and handed him the phone. "Lana wants to talk to you."

He searched Maggie's face, but she didn't look as if Lana had reassured her very much.

Damn, what had she told her? "Do I need to bring her to the hospital tonight?" he asked Lana.

"No. As I told Maggie, there's really nothing we can do at this point. She needs to try to calm down and take it easy. Rest, and try to get some sleep."

Tucker looked at Maggie. "Calm down? I don't think that's happening, but I'll try."

"Will you be able to come with her in the morning?"

"Absolutely."

"Good, she needs your support right now. I'm going to do a test on her HCG level tomorrow, and that might tell us a little more. The levels should go up exponentially at this stage of pregnancy. It will be another one or two weeks or so before we'll be able to see the baby on an ultrasound."

"And there's nothing I can do to help her? Nothing you can do?"

"Nothing other than try to reassure her. There are any number of reasons for spotting at this stage. Most of them don't mean she's having a miscarriage."

"But she could be."

Lana hesitated, then said, "Yes, it's possible. I'm sorry, Tucker."

He thanked her and hung up, setting the phone on the bedside table. Then he put his arms around Maggie and pulled her close. She didn't resist. Her arms went around him and she laid her head on his shoulder. Her cheek was damp against his skin. "I can't do this again," she whispered. "I can't lose another baby."

"You aren't going to lose it. Lana said there were all kinds of reasons for spotting."

"One of which is a miscarriage."

It was a fact he couldn't deny. They both had to face the possibility. "I wish I could promise you that the baby will be fine, but obviously, I can't. But I can promise you that whatever happens, you won't be going through this alone. You're not getting rid of me, Maggie."

She was quiet for a long moment, then pulled back and looked at him. "Why are you so good to me?"

"Because I love you." He kissed her mouth. "Don't even think about going back to the other bedroom. You're sleeping with me."

She didn't argue. She got into bed with him and let him wrap her in his arms. "Tucker?"

"Yeah?"

"I'm glad you're here with me."

"Me, too. Now try to get some sleep."

"I can't. All I can think about is what happened before. I don't ever want to hurt like that again."

"I don't want you to, either." He paused. Trying to comfort her, he blurted out, "Maggie, I'm hoping and praying you won't lose this baby. But if it happens… We could try again. On purpose this time."

She started crying again and he cursed himself for being a fool.

CHAPTER TWENTY-THREE

"I DIDN'T MEAN—I know it wouldn't make up for losing this one, but— Damn, Maggie, don't cry. I'm an idiot. I'm sorry; forget I said anything." He patted her back. "Don't cry."

"It's so sweet," she said, finally managing to stop leaking tears. "You're so sweet. I know what you meant and I appreciate it, Tucker. I really do. But you don't have to do that. You've done enough for me."

He groaned. "You really don't get it."

Yes, she did. She understood perfectly. Tucker was a wonderful, kind man who wanted her to be happy. "You told Lana you were coming with me in the morning. You don't need to. I appreciate the offer, but I can go without you."

"You're not going alone. So do me a favor and don't argue about it. Get some sleep."

"All right." She was an emotional wreck.

Sleep could only help. "Tucker? Thank you for being here for me."

"There's no place else I'd rather be than with you." He kissed her forehead and closed his arms around her. She felt safe…and loved. Was it an illusion or did he really love her, after all?

Maggie fell asleep pondering that question. And dreamed of Tucker and a sweet baby boy.

TUCKER INSISTED ON standing beside her and holding her hand while they waited for Lana to return with the HCG level test results. She didn't fight him since she'd been up since dawn and the waiting left her white-knuckled and desperate to know something. And hollowly uncertain of what she'd do if Lana confirmed she would lose the baby.

The door opened and Lana came in holding a manila folder Maggie assumed was her records. "Your HCG level indicates you're still pregnant, so that's good."

Hope bubbled in her heart. "I'm not having a miscarriage?"

"Unfortunately, we can't rule that out entirely. What we might do is take another level in forty-eight hours and then again forty-eight hours after that. If the HCG levels continue to increase that's a good sign that the pregnancy is progressing normally."

"So all we can do is wait?" Tucker asked.

"I know it's hard. But honestly, at this point there isn't much else to do." She smiled at him, then turned to Maggie. "Can you tell me anything else about your symptoms? Last night all you mentioned was the bleeding. Did you notice any more, or did it get heavier?"

"Nothing since last night. It was just the blood. Not very much, but it freaked me out."

"I understand. Last night did you have any cramping?"

Maggie shook her head. "No. Just the spotting." Lana wrote something down and Maggie asked her one of the questions that had been bothering her. "We had sex yesterday. Could that have caused it?"

Lana looked up and gave her a reassuring smile. "It might have caused some bleeding, but if you are having a miscarriage that wouldn't be the cause. However, to be safe, I would refrain until we know more about how the pregnancy is progressing."

Or about how it isn't, Maggie thought glumly.

"Don't worry," Tucker said. "We'll do whatever we need to."

"Cheer up. It's not for the duration. Just until we know more."

Unless she filed. The thought of not only losing the baby but of losing Tucker, too, depressed the hell out of her. To never make love with him again, or see him, or have him to talk to and tell about her day, to spar with, or even to hang out and watch the tube. No, she couldn't bear to think about that. Not on top of everything else.

She made an appointment to come in the day after tomorrow and then she and Tucker left. She thought about returning to work, but Tucker had a fit, so she didn't. After lecturing her about resting and taking care of herself, Tucker left for the office. She felt a pang of guilt knowing he'd been putting off taking care of his business yet again because of her.

She should do what she'd been talking about for the last several days and go file the papers for the divorce. That's what she should do.... But she didn't. Instead, she crawled into bed— Tucker's bed—and took a nap.

That night and the next day, Maggie carefully did not bring up divorce, and neither did Tucker. She went back to work on a limited basis, trying hard not to run to the bathroom every few minutes to check that everything was all right.

The second test set her mind a little more at rest, and Lana said the third, in two more days, should make them all breathe easier.

Once the pregnancy was far enough along, in about another week or two, they would take an ultrasound and continue to monitor its progress that way. They left the date for the ultrasound up in the air, though, since Lana was so close to delivery. Lana had said she wanted to do the test herself and insisted that it wouldn't be a problem, even if she'd had her baby. Even though she told herself not to count on anything, as more time passed Maggie began to feel cautiously optimistic.

The evening after the second HCG test she and Tucker went to see Grace and her mother. Maggie had deliberately stayed away, afraid that seeing Grace again would only make her feel worse, but she missed her so much she couldn't stand it. She'd kept an eye on Carol and Grace through CPS, and she'd heard they were doing well. But eventually, she had to see for herself that the baby was happy. Carol had agreed enthusiastically when Maggie had called the night before and asked if she and Tucker could come see them.

"You're sure this is a good time?" Maggie asked, as Carol showed them in.

"Anytime is a good time for you two." She smiled to include Tucker. "I know I have you to thank that Grace is so happy and healthy." She looked down at the baby in her arms and smiled. "Not to mention I know you're the one who helped me get me that job, Maggie."

"That was just luck that I heard about the cleaners needing help."

"But you didn't have to tell me about it. You know I wouldn't have gotten Grace back if I didn't have a job." Grace held out her arms, wanting to go to Maggie. Carol laughed and handed her over so Maggie could sit with her. "She's missed you."

"I missed her, too." Maggie looked at the blue-eyed, blond little girl cooing and babbling in her lap and felt her heart swell. "She's grown so much."

Carol nodded. "At this age even a few of weeks makes a difference."

Grace was obviously thriving. And Carol looked like a totally different person from the sad, desperate young woman Maggie had first met at the police station.

"Grace looks great," Tucker said. "How's she doing with day care?"

"She seems to like it. I had a hard time leaving

her after just getting her back, but the hours are good at the cleaners. And her caregiver at the day care loves her."

They talked a while longer and played with Grace until it was clearly her bedtime. Maggie stood to leave and a wave of dizziness hit her so fast and hard, she nearly fell. If it hadn't been for Tucker grabbing her she thought she might have gone to ground. "I'm okay."

"The hell you are. Sit down. No, lie down. Do you mind if she stretches out on the couch?" he asked Carol.

"No, of course not. Are you all right, Maggie?" she asked anxiously. "Is there something I can do? Get you a glass of water?"

"I'm fine," Maggie said, but she did sit down. "Tucker's overreacting."

"She's not fine, she's pregnant," Tucker told Carol. "And she's supposed to be taking it easy."

Maggie scowled at him. "I have been taking it easy. I only worked a half day today, and the chief has me on desk duty."

Carol went to the kitchen, returning with a glass of water, which she gave to Maggie. Maggie drank it and felt better. This time when she stood, the dizziness didn't return. Tucker insisted he would bring the car to the building since the lot had been full and they'd parked some distance away.

"I envy you," Carol said softly after he left.

Startled, Maggie looked at her. "Why?"

"Because you're having your child with the man you love. And he's obviously a good man who loves you very much."

"Things aren't always what they seem."

"Oh, don't get me wrong. I wouldn't take another chance of being with someone who would hurt my baby. Not ever. But if I could have a man like that look at me the way Tucker does you, I'd feel very lucky."

THE DAYS UNTIL the ultrasound passed slowly for Maggie as she suspected they did for Tucker, although the fact that the third hormone-level test showed increasingly elevated levels of HCG helped tremendously. Maggie still hadn't brought up the divorce. She'd decided to wait until after the ultrasound to sort that all out. Maybe it was selfish of her, but she needed Tucker right now. She wasn't sure she'd have made it through without him.

Tucker didn't seem in any hurry to get rid of her. He wouldn't let her sleep in the other bedroom, but convinced her she slept better in his bed. And since she slept like a baby every night wrapped in his arms, she couldn't exactly argue.

Lana and Gabe had their baby, a healthy baby boy they named after his father. Lana still insisted she wanted to do the ultrasound and scheduled it for the week after she brought the baby home. She said baby Gabriel would be fine with his father for the hour or so it would take her to run the test.

Finally the day of the ultrasound dawned, when Maggie was about seven and a half weeks pregnant. Lana had told them that she expected to see a perfectly healthy pregnancy, since all the tests had been good and Maggie had experienced no worrisome symptoms after the initial spotting. In fact, she'd been sick every morning, which also made her hopeful.

Maggie clutched Tucker's hand while the technician spread gel over her stomach. Lana took the ultrasound device from the tech and placed it on Maggie's stomach. Maggie shut her eyes and prayed. Very shortly, Lana spoke. "There. There's the baby, and there's the heartbeat. Maggie, don't you want to look?"

Her eyes had flown open when she'd heard the word *heartbeat*. She stared at the screen along with Tucker. "Can you see it, Tucker?"

"I think so." He didn't sound too sure, though.

She didn't want to admit it, but she couldn't really tell much. "Are you sure you see a heart-beat?" she asked Lana. "I can't see anything."

"I'm sure," Lana said. "I've had a bit more practice than you. It's hard to see this early." She placed a pointer on the area she wanted them to look at.

"I see it now," Maggie said, trying not to cry. "You think the baby is all right?"

"I do," Lana said.

"I can see it," Tucker said. "Wow, that's so cool. It's so tiny."

"Very cool," Lana agreed. "We'll do another one in a few weeks, but I don't think you need to worry. I think the spotting was simply spotting and nothing to be concerned about. You can resume all your normal activities."

"Everything?" Tucker asked.

Lana laughed. "Well, I wouldn't recommend skydiving, but pretty much anything else is all right."

"Does she still need to take it easy?"

"Only if she feels bad. I think things are going to be just fine." Lana patted his shoulder, then smiled at Maggie and left the room.

She and the baby were going to be all right.

Along with huge relief, Maggie felt a growing depression. There was no reason for she and Tucker to stay together now. Except that she loved him and wanted to be with him.

But what if he really did love her and she'd just been too stubbornly sure she'd messed up his life to see it? She thought about the past months, especially the weeks since Grace had gone back to live with her mother. Tucker had been there for her because he wanted to be. You couldn't fake something like that. And if he'd loved Grace, how would he feel about a child of his own? Was it fair to him to take the choice of raising his child with her away from him? Because she had decided he couldn't possibly want to be with her?

Didn't she owe them—she, Tucker and the baby—a chance to be a family?

CHAPTER TWENTY-FOUR

"TUCKER, WHEN WE GET home we need to talk."
She planned to approach him cautiously. Start
with the idea of not filing for divorce just yet,
since he seemed to want to experience the pregnancy with her. Later she'd worry about what
to do once the baby was born. Maybe by then
she'd have a clearer idea of whether he really
was in love with her or just bent on doing the
right thing.

Tucker shot her a glance she couldn't read.
"My thoughts exactly. I took the rest of the day
off."

"I don't want your work to suffer because of
me. You've already missed a lot."

"Don't worry about that. I've rescheduled
everything and can catch up next week."

Once at home they went to the den. Maggie
sat on the couch, but Tucker didn't. Instead he
stood by the fireplace, rearranging stuff on the

mantel. "I've been thinking—" Maggie began but Tucker interrupted, turning to look at her.

"I know what you're going to say."

"I don't think you do."

Tucker nodded. "Oh, yeah, I do. You're going to bring up filing again. Because the baby is fine, et cetera, et cetera. But I want to have my say before you do."

"I wasn't exactly—"

"Maggie, are you going to let me talk or not?"

He sounded so stern it made her want to giggle. *Must be the hormones,* she thought. But he also seemed very agitated, so she shrugged and decided to let him go first. "Okay. Go ahead."

He didn't. Instead, he paced the room. She watched him a moment then said, "Tucker? I thought you were going to talk."

"I'm working on it." He came to a halt before her. "I've been trying to figure out a way to convince you I love you. I know I screwed up not telling you before you told me you were pregnant. But I can't change that."

"Tucker, let me—"

He shot her a "don't mess with me" look, so she relented.

"At first I thought about having my dad tell you what we talked about at the Scarlet Parrot earlier on the same day you told me about the baby. Delilah could have told you we were there. But I knew you'd think my dad would do whatever I asked him to, and he would. So that was out. Besides, I need to prove it to you myself."

She started to speak but he raised a finger. "I'm not finished." He put his hands in his pockets and paced again. "Then it occurred to me. You're a cop. You're a logical woman and when presented with the facts you'll listen. I'm not a trial lawyer but I took trial advocacy in law school. So I know how to present a case. And that's what I intend to do."

She stared at him for a moment. "You're presenting a case that you love me?"

"Yes." He held up a finger. "First piece of evidence, what have I said every time you mentioned filing for divorce? You started talking about it even before Grace's mother came back. When we had our date and I kissed you. Do you remember what I said?"

"Not exactly. I remember you talked me out of it."

"That's right. Just like I did every time you brought it up. After Grace left, I said we didn't need to rush into filing. When what I really meant was that I didn't want a divorce at all."

"That's not what you said."

"Out of order. I'm not finished presenting the evidence."

Maggie pressed her lips together, smothering a laugh. "Fine. Go ahead."

"All right. Here's another piece of evidence. Have I ever referred to us having sex as anything but making love?"

"I don't know. I don't remember."

"I remember and I haven't. Because it isn't just sex between us, it's making love."

She'd been a cop long enough to know when a person was lying. She'd bet everything she had, but most especially her heart, that Tucker was telling the truth. She got up to go to him but he stopped her words with his fingers on her lips. Then he gathered her hands in his and looked into her eyes.

"Maggie, I love you. I want you. I want to spend my life with you. I want to have babies with you. This one, another one, more if you want. I believe I can convince you I'm telling you the truth when I say I love you. If you'll give me a chance to prove it." He kissed her hands, then smiled at her. "But what I don't know is how you feel about me. It seems like every time I start to think you might love me, you bring up divorce."

Her heart had turned to mush as he spoke. She shook one of her hands loose and put it on his cheek. Gazed at him lovingly. "Are you finished presenting your case?"

"Did I mention I love you?"

Maggie nodded. "Yes, you did."

"Then I'm finished."

"Do you know what I was going to say at the beginning of this conversation?" He shook his head. "I was going to suggest we wait on filing until after the baby was born. And I planned to keep putting it off until I knew whether you loved me or you were staying with me because you thought it was the right thing."

"Really?" He looked so suspicious, she laughed.

"I don't want a divorce, Tucker. I only kept bringing it up because I believed that was what was best for you. I didn't want to trap you. I didn't want you to stay married to me simply because it was the right thing. I wanted you to love me."

"I told you from the beginning that I married you because I wanted to. I finally figured out I've been falling for you from the day we said our vows. Maybe before that."

"I love you, too. I have for a long time. For so long, I can't remember not loving you."

He pulled her into his arms. "Those are the words I've been waiting to hear." He kissed her, long, slow and loving. "I love you, Maggie."

"I know," she said, and laughed as he scooped her into his arms and carried her to the bedroom.

She looped her arms around his neck and strung kisses along his jaw. "There's something we need to do first."

He paid no attention, depositing her on the bed with great care. "Tucker, I mean it. We need to take care of something before we make love."

He had his shirt halfway unbuttoned but he paused and looked at her. "If you tell me you're having second thoughts—"

"No, nothing like that. But...I'd like to say our vows again. This time for real." She waited a little anxiously, unsure whether he'd think the idea was silly.

He smiled and sat on the bed. "Do you want to go first or should I?"

"I'll go first."

"Give me your hands."

She put her hands in his. "Tucker, when I first asked you to marry me I thought you'd be the perfect temporary husband. But it didn't take me very long to discover that you are the perfect husband for me and that I want our marriage to last the rest of our lives. You're my best friend, and my lover, and I want very much for you to be my husband. For always. Because I love you more than I can say."

He smiled at her, such a tender expression in his eyes she thought she'd drown in them. Tears started in her own eyes as he spoke. "Maggie, when you first cooked up this scheme I thought you were nuts. I told myself I'd marry you to help you out. I didn't realize that it would take me about a week to fall totally in love with you. So here's to crazy schemes and to the one woman in the world who is making my dreams come true. Dreams I didn't even know I had until I married you. I promise to love you, cherish you, and every year on the anniversary of the day you asked me to marry you, I promise to dream up something just as crazy for us to do together."

Maggie laughed through her tears. "I love you. You are such a nut."

He took her face in his hands and kissed her soundly. "I love you, too, Mrs. Jones. And that makes us perfect together."

About seven months later

TUCKER BENT DOWN to kiss the soft hair on his newborn son's head. "He's so amazing. He's incredible." He kissed Maggie and sat on the bed beside her. "And so is his mother."

"Isn't he perfect?" Love swamped her as she looked at her baby. "Look, his fingers are so tiny." She picked up one of his tiny fists and kissed it. "Do you want to hold him?"

"Absolutely." He held out his arms and she transferred the baby into them. "What are we going to name him? I have an idea if you don't."

She stroked the baby's cheek. "He looks like you, Tucker. And what makes you think I don't have any ideas?"

"Oh, maybe because you refused to discuss names the entire pregnancy."

"I do have an idea. But let's hear yours first."

"I thought since Grace is the reason we married in the first place, we should name the baby after her. But I'm not naming my son Grace."

Maggie laughed. "No, I think the other kids might tease him if we did that."

"Let's name him Davis, for Grace's last name."

"You must be a mind reader." She put her

hand on the baby's head and smiled at Tucker and their son. "Welcome to the world, Davis Tucker Jones."

* * * * *

*Look for LAST WOLF WATCHING
by Rhyannon Byrd—the exciting conclusion
in the BLOODRUNNERS miniseries
from Silhouette Nocturne.*

*Follow Michaela and Brody on their fierce
journey to find the truth and face the demons
from the past, as they reach the heart of the
battle between the Runners and the rogues.*

*Here is a sneak preview of book three,
LAST WOLF WATCHING.*

Michaela squinted, struggling to see through the impenetrable darkness. Everyone looked toward the Elders, but she knew Brody Carter still watched her. Michaela could feel the power of his gaze. Its heat. Its strength. And something that felt strangely like anger, though he had no reason to have any emotion toward her. Strangers from different worlds, brought together beneath the heavy silver moon on a night made for hell itself. That was their only connection.

The second she finished that thought, she knew it was a lie. But she couldn't deal with it now. Not tonight. Not when her whole world balanced on the edge of destruction.

Willing her backbone to keep her upright, Michaela Doucet focused on the towering blaze of a roaring bonfire that rose from the far side of the clearing, its orange flames burning with maniacal zeal against the inky black curtain of the night. Many of the Lycans had already shifted into their preternatural shapes, their fur-covered bodies standing like monstrous shadows at the edges of the forest as they waited with restless expectancy for her brother.

Her nineteen-year-old brother, Max, had been attacked by a rogue werewolf—a Lycan who preyed upon humans for food. Max had been bitten in the attack, which meant he was no longer human, but a breed of creature that existed between the two worlds of man and beast, much like the Bloodrunners themselves.

The Elders parted, and two hulking shapes emerged from the trees. In their wolf forms, the Lycans stood over seven feet tall, their legs bent at an odd angle as they stalked forward. They each held a thick chain that had been wound around their inside wrists, the twin lengths leading back into the shadows. The Lycans had taken no more than a few steps when they jerked on the chains, and her brother appeared.

Bound like an animal.

Biting at her trembling lower lip, she glanced left, then right, surprised to see that others had joined her. Now the Bloodrunners and their family and friends stood as a united force against the Silvercrest pack, which had yet to accept the fact that something sinister was eating away at its foundation—something that would rip down the protective walls that separated their world from the humans'. It occurred to Michaela that loyalties were being announced tonight—a separation made between those who would stand with the Runners in their fight against the rogues and those who blindly supported the pack's refusal to face reality. But all she could focus on was her brother. Max looked so hurt…so terrified.

"Leave him alone," she screamed, her soft-soled, black satin slip-ons struggling for purchase in the damp earth as she rushed toward Max, only to find herself lifted off the ground when a hard, heavily muscled arm clamped around her waist from behind, pulling her clear off her feet. "Damn it, let me down!" she snarled, unable to take her eyes off her brother as the golden-eyed Lycan kicked him.

Mindless with heartache and rage, Michaela clawed at the arm holding her, kicking her heels against whatever part of her captor's legs she could reach. "Stop it," a deep, husky voice grunted in her ear. "You're not helping him by losing it. I give you my word he'll survive the ceremony, but you have to keep it together."

"Nooooo!" she screamed, too hysterical to listen to reason. "You're monsters! All of you! Look what you've done to him! How dare you! *How dare you!*"

The arm tightened with a powerful flex of muscle, cinching her waist. Her breath sucked in on a sharp, wailing gasp.

"Shut up before you get both yourself and your brother killed. I will *not* let that happen. Do you understand me?" her captor growled, shaking her so hard that her teeth clicked together. "Do you understand me, Doucet?"

"Damn it," she cried, stricken as she watched one of the guards grab Max by his hair. Around them Lycans huffed and growled as they watched the spectacle, while others outright howled for the show to begin.

"That's enough!" the voice seethed in her ear. "They'll tear you apart before you even reach him, and I'll be damned if I'm going to stand here and watch you die."

Suddenly, through the haze of fear and agony and outrage in her mind, she finally recognized who'd caught her. *Brody*.

He held her in his arms, her body locked

against his powerful form, her back to the burning heat of his chest. A low, keening sound of anguish tore through her, and her head dropped forward as hoarse sobs of pain ripped from her throat. "Let me go. I have to help him. *Please*," she begged brokenly, knowing only that she needed to get to Max. "Let me go, Brody."

He muttered something against her hair, his breath warm against her scalp, and Michaela could have sworn it was a single word…. But she must have heard wrong. She was too upset. Too furious. Too terrified. She must be out of her mind.

Because it sounded as if he'd quietly snarled the word *never*.

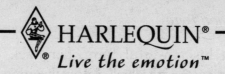

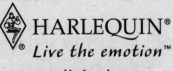

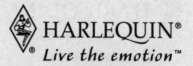

HARLEQUIN®
INTRIGUE®

BREATHTAKING ROMANTIC SUSPENSE

Shared dangers and passions lead to electrifying
romance and heart-stopping suspense!

Every month, you'll meet six new heroes
who are guaranteed to make your spine tingle
and your pulse pound. With them you'll enter
into the exciting world of Harlequin Intrigue—
where your life is on the line
and so is your heart!

THAT'S INTRIGUE—
ROMANTIC SUSPENSE
AT ITS BEST!

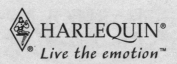

HARLEQUIN®
Live the emotion™

Harlequin® Historical
Historical Romantic Adventure!

Imagine a time of chivalrous knights and unconventional ladies, roguish rakes and impetuous heiresses, rugged cowboys and spirited frontierswomen—— these rich and vivid tales will capture your imagination!

Harlequin Historical… they're too good to miss!

HHDIR06